AUG 1 8 1986

2 88 00368420 4

O9-ABF-270

Get Out of My Face

Get Out of My Face

David Masterton

ATHENEUM   1991   NEW YORK

Maxwell Macmillan Canada *Toronto*
Maxwell Macmillan International
New York   Oxford   Singapore   Sydney

Copyright © 1991 by David Stuart Masterton

All rights reserved. No part of this book may be reproduced or transmitted in any form or by any means, electronic or mechanical, including photocopying, recording, or by any information storage and retrieval system, without permission in writing from the publisher.

Atheneum
Macmillan Publishing Company
866 Third Avenue
New York, NY 10022

Maxwell Macmillan Canada, Inc.
1200 Eglinton Avenue East
Suite 200
Don Mills, Ontario M3C 3N1

Macmillan Publishing Company is part of the Maxwell Communication Group of Companies.

First edition
Printed in the United States of America
1   2   3   4   5   6   7   8   9   10

Library of Congress Cataloging-in-Publication Data
Masterton, David.
    Get out of my face / David Masterton. — 1st ed.
        p.   cm.
    Summary: Fifteen-year-old Kate finds her adjustment to her new twelve-year-old stepbrother, who is obnoxious and antagonistic, made even more difficult when they have to help each other survive on a dangerous wilderness journey.
    ISBN 0–689–31675–5
    [1. Stepfamilies—Fiction.   2. Survival—Fiction.]   I. Title.
PZ7.M423954Ge   1991
[Fic]—dc20   90-24096

FOR LAURA, HEATHER, AND MICHAEL

Gift (13 25)

Macmillan

10-16-91

M394g

Contents

The Disaster

The Oskeet River:

10:06 A.M., THURSDAY, JULY 12

With his sister, Linda, in the bow and his stepsister, Kate, in the stern, Joey Morgan lolled in the middle of the canoe, his back against the strut bar, arms dangling over the side, as smug as a rich kid on his own hundred-foot yacht.

"Come on, Kate! I thought you were a pro. This wreck is poking along. Where are your muscles, girl," he said.

Kate Evans closed her eyes and told herself to stay calm. She didn't want another fight with Joey this morning. Opening her eyes, she saw Joey grinning at her. He had turned halfway around, giving her the full pleasure of his orange T shirt with its slogan GET OUT OF MY FACE printed in large blue letters across the front.

That shirt says it all, thought Kate. That's the kind of kid he is. And only Joey would wear purple sunglasses that are so big they keep sliding down his nose. As she watched, Joey slid the sunglasses back up as if it was the most important and most luxurious thing he could do in the whole world.

"Getting tired, girl? Have to take a nap to keep up your strength?"

3

That did it. He was asking for it.

"You should talk about napping and muscles. With those puny arms, it's a wonder your mother doesn't spoon-feed you," Kate said as she dug her paddle deep into the river.

She liked the way the paddle cut through the water, the spray lifting into the sunburned July air. The mid-morning sun was reflecting off the river like a thousand bright oncoming headlights, making her wish she had remembered her own glasses. Squinting was giving her a big fat headache.

"I'd rather have puny arms than those boa constrictor ones you have," Joey said laughing.

He knows he got me in my sore spot, that's why he's cackling like a hyena, Kate told herself. My genes would have to mix me up with a gorilla! Sure, long arms are great for swimming and basketball, but they don't look feminine, not even when I try to hide them in sweatshirts and jeans. And anyway, who can wear those things when it's eighty-four degrees?

In her halter top and shorts, Kate was sure her long legs and arms made her look like a giraffe. She had always been the tallest girl in her class. Even now at fifteen, she was taller than most of the boys.

Kate dipped her paddle into the river, and scooping water into the air, flung it at Joey, drenching his face and sunglasses.

"Hey!" he yelled. "You jerk! What did you do that for?"

"Just thought you needed something cool and refreshing," she said laughing, feeling better that she had soaked him.

Joey lunged at her. "Think you're funny? I'll show you something funny!" Kate didn't move her legs fast enough, and he grabbed her by the foot.

Kate kept spraying him with water, and Joey kept pulling at her. He was turned completely around, facing her now, up on his knees. Each time he jerked her foot, he laughed his hyena cackle. He plans on doing something nasty, Kate told herself. Things haven't changed one inch between us.

The canoe was rocking furiously back and forth from the tug-of-war. Linda Morgan, sitting in the bow, holding on tightly to the sides, was yelling at them to stop, yelling something about rocks. But with Joey wrenching at her sneaker, trying to get it off, Kate was only half listening. She knew Joey would throw her sneaker into the river, and she wasn't going to let him. She wasn't going to let this boy get the best of her.

By the time Linda's screams broke through to Kate's consciousness, it was too late. She saw the rock a second before the canoe slammed against it, the blow tipping them dangerously to the side, spinning the canoe out of control.

That quickly, they were in the middle of rapids. The river had changed suddenly. No longer a slow, peaceful stream, it was now a monster, raging down between steep, rocky hills.

Though she and her father had never canoed the south branch of the Oskeet before, Kate knew about the rapids. She had seen them marked on the geological survey map. But with Joey bugging her, she had missed the signs of the river picking up speed, misjudging how near they actually were.

The river roller-coastered over and between boulders the size of cars, and they went along with it. After they hit the first rock, Kate straightened them out enough that they shot past the next three. All they could do now was hold on to their paddles and the sides of the canoe as tightly as possible, and pray they would thread their way between the rocks. But Kate wasn't sure praying was going to be enough. They were now lurching to the right, the rear end of the canoe swinging out and around, trying to turn them sideways, propelled by the force of the rapids.

Kate was more scared than she had ever been in her life. Her heart boomed in her ears. She sat squeezing the paddle and staring at Joey. He was still facing her. His hands, which seconds before had been pulling her sneaker, were now clamped to the sides of the canoe. His face was drained white, his mouth wide open. Kate couldn't tell if he was saying something. The noise of the rapids was so loud she couldn't hear anything but the water roaring all around them. It was then, over his shoulder, that she saw straight ahead a boulder twice as big as all the others.

Kate pushed and dug her paddle frantically against the smaller rocks, trying to turn the canoe. But all she could do was keep it from hitting broadside. The canoe hit the boulder on the right of the bow, the shock knocking Kate out of her seat and with a back-wrenching jerk over the side and into the river.

Kate held on to her paddle, jamming it against the rock as she went under, her head just missing the rock. The rapids carried her down, spinning her and plunging her deep, then pushing her up to the surface, almost as though it knew she needed air. She caught sight of Linda once, a flash of Linda's yellow top off to her right. She didn't see Joey at all.

There wasn't time to think about anything. The rapids were jerking her up and down and sideways like she was a string puppet, the sand on the river bottom scraping her legs and arms, and the rocks jolting her to her teeth as the water threw her against them.

Her entire body was in pain. Her muscles barely moved as she fought her way up to the surface for air. She was getting weak. She knew she couldn't keep going much longer.

Kate took a last, quick gulp of air before being plunged down again. But it wasn't enough. Her lungs felt like they were ready to burst her chest open. She tried to get back to the surface, but couldn't find it. She didn't know which way to go. The rapids kept twisting her around and pulling her down. Keeping her mouth closed became the hardest thing she had ever done. She wanted to open it and suck in buckets and buckets of air.

Kate's head felt strange, as if a soft pillow were being gently pressed over her face. She couldn't breathe. She seemed to be slipping into a dream, a dream about silver lights shining up at her from the bottom of a dark hole. She knew she was drowning.

Her eyes were almost closed when her feet touched something, something hard. Automatically, not thinking, unable to think, her legs stretched and pushed with what strength was left in them. And then suddenly, sparkling with sunlight, the surface of the river broke around her.

Kate gasped for air. The pain in her chest was awful. But nothing ever felt so good to her as breathing air. The river was still flowing fast, but the rapids were behind her. She floated with the current, sucking air in through her mouth, waiting for enough strength to swim. Finally, the pain in her chest lessened and she was able to do a limp sidestroke. She swam to a dead tree sticking out from the bank and grabbed one of the branches.

Kate hung there off the end of the tree for a long while, trying to shake the feeling of weakness that went right through her. As she looked back upriver, all she could see of the rapids were the gray boulders and the spray that seemed to hang over them like a white frothy curtain. Kate knew she would feel better if she stayed there, draped off the end of the tree a bit longer, resting, letting the water soothe her body, taking away more of the weakness she felt; but she couldn't. She was too worried about Joey and Linda. She knew they hadn't made it through the rapids or she would have seen them by now. That meant they were still back somewhere among the rocks, and maybe hurt. She had to find them.

From Kate Evans's Diary:

T H U R S D A Y,   M A Y   3

*L*ast night, we were invited to dinner at Mrs. Morgan's. She's a widow, Dad told me, whose husband died in a plane crash three years ago. Hearing about things like that gives me goose bumps. It must be horrible for someone to die like that. And when it's someone you care about how do you keep it from eating you up inside? I don't know what I'd do if Dad died. He's been just about my whole family most of my life.

Anyway, Dad and Mrs. Morgan have been dating a long time, close to a year, but I never thought about it much, cause Dad has dated other women before her. I never asked him anything about her. She's a woman he goes out with, that's all.

Before tonight, I met Mrs. Morgan maybe twice to say "Hi," when she and Dad stopped at the apartment. The only thing I really knew about her was that she had two kids about my age.

I didn't want to go to dinner at her house because a great video came on MTV at eight o'clock, but Dad said we were going, so that was that.

The house is blue and vanilla with a tiny front porch, a two-car garage, and marigolds growing around a tree in the front yard. It's a typical house for Brewster, a town about eight or nine miles from here in Warren. At the front door, Dad put his hand on my shoulder and said to be nice.

When am I ever not nice? When I meet a bratty kid. And that was Joey, burping and picking his nose. He's a squirt next to me. Maybe he's five feet tall, while I'm flirting with five foot seven. To be fair, I suppose his height is about average for his age. He just turned twelve last month, so I'm three years older. Anyway, he definitely has that look of prepuberty meanness that boys get when their hormones are all scrunched up, ready to explode.

His sister, Linda, is almost a year older than me. Pretty and petite, she is at the most only three inches taller than Joey. And where I gab all the time, she was so quiet she made me nervous. I felt like a giant next to her, not dainty or feminine at all.

Neither of them seemed to want me there any more than I wanted to be there. Linda only gave me half smiles. And when they sat me across from Joey, I had to watch him stick his finger up his nose, then pull it out and show me his prize find. Sickening.

Always the girl who lets people know what she thinks whether they want to know or not, I let the juvenile delinquent have it.

"You are so disgusting," I said loud enough so everyone heard me. "I never met such a disgusting kid. You belong with pigs."

Mrs. Morgan and Dad had been talking quietly and

laughing at the other end of the table, their heads close together, not paying any attention to us kids. Now they were paying tons of attention. I could feel their silent disapproval.

"Oink! Oink!" Joey said with a wide smirk across his face.

I'd tried to be nice to him, asking him about school and about soccer. Dad had told me Joey played soccer. But the boy just mumbled that I should butt out, that girls "talked stupid" about sports. His saying that bugged me because I like sports, but I left him alone the way he wanted and tried talking with Linda.

Even if she was quiet, she was at least friendlier, and she didn't pick her nose once, which was a big plus. We found out that we liked the same music groups, and so were getting along okay. Not instant buddies, but what do you expect when you're plopped down next to a stranger.

Then Joey started acting really gross. Jeez was he gross. He was dipping lima beans into his mashed potatoes, then sticking them to his upper lip so they looked like they were coming out his nose. I tried to wish Mrs. Morgan or Dad to look up and see him, but they were too busy talking. It was all I could do to ignore him and keep yakking to Linda. She was telling me about a really cute boy in her math class, when Joey made this loud belch. I knew he did it on purpose cause he was looking cross-eyed right at me, and had a big grin on his face.

"You are so gross!" I actually shouted across the table at him. I was so angry, I couldn't stop myself.

"Kate, stop that yelling!" Dad's voice boomed at me.

Dad's a big man. He's six foot four and he used to play football. So when he stands up and talks loudly like that he scares people. But I know Dad doesn't mean to be scary. He's really very kind.

"I've tried being nice to him, Dad, but he's crude. He picks his nose and burps, and keeps butting in when I'm talking. I'm sorry I yelled. But I just don't like him. If you want, I'll go and sit in the living room away from him," I said. I was angry. I hadn't done anything really wrong, but I was the one leaving the table. It was the brat's fault. He should have been the one to leave and go to a dungeon or someplace where slimy worms would crawl all over him.

I was in the living room just long enough to flop on the couch when Mrs. Morgan came and sat down beside me. I was expecting Dad to come and lecture me, but this was worse—the kid's mother. My dinner started doing flips in my stomach. What was she going to do?

All she did was take my hand, hold it, and smile at me. She was very pretty, with short blond hair and big green eyes. She didn't wear much makeup, just lipstick and a bit of rouge. She was small like Linda, so I felt like a giraffe next to her.

"Kate, I know Joey wasn't very nice to you. He's that way with girls, particularly girls who are friendly with Linda. Ever since his father died, he's become very attached to his sister and, unfortunately, gets jealous if she pays attention to someone else." She said this with such a frown, wrinkles popped out on her forehead, making her look older all of a sudden.

"I guess I wasn't very patient with him," I said, embarrassed that I'd made a scene. I'd overreacted as usual. "I don't have a brother, so I'm not very used to boys. They're so different from girls."

Mrs. Morgan smiled then very prettily, the wrinkles disappearing, and said, "They sure are. Come on back to the dining room and have some ice cream. Joey's gone over to his friend's house to play video games. Your dad said you have to go back home soon, so come and spend some time with Linda."

The Oskeet River:

*H*urrying to pull herself up the bank, Kate slipped in the mud, banging her knee on a root. "Great going, Kate!" she said out loud, angry for having fallen. She winced as she pushed herself up off the ground.

As Kate limped back toward the rapids, the roar of the water seemed to approach ear-bursting levels. Not able to hear anything but the water, she almost passed right by Jocy. Only by chance, out of the corner of her eye, did she spot his orange shirt against the rocks. He was clinging to a tree branch caught between two boulders, screaming words she couldn't hear. His eyes seemed to be bulging out of his head, and she thought she saw blood trickling down his cheek.

Seeing how bad Joey looked, Kate knew he couldn't hold on much longer. And as little as she liked the idea, knew she was the only one who could help him.

"If I don't help you, you'll go and drown just to spite me, won't you," she yelled at his unhearing, anxious face.

But how was she going to get to him? He was out too far for her to reach him from the bank, and the water was too rough and rocky to swim.

The only way to save him was if he let go of the tree branch. The river would then carry him away from the rocks, and there would be a chance for her to swim out and grab him. Kate knew she would have to judge the distance just right, or Joey would be swept past her. If she missed him, he would drown. No, she couldn't tell him to let go. She couldn't take the chance of missing him.

"Why didn't you ever learn to swim, you jerk?" she yelled into the noise of the rapids. Then, quieter, to herself, she asked, "What am I going to do?"

She stood there, staring at him, frozen by indecision. Then, as she watched horrified, Joey's hands slipped off the branch. Twice he grabbed frantically for the tree but the rapids were too strong. She saw him yell something before disappearing beneath the water.

Kate ran as fast as she could along the bank, as fast as the mud and the tree roots and her banged-up knee would let her. She saw his head break through the surface of the water every few seconds, his arms and legs thrashing. She remembered him saying there was nothing to swimming, knowing full well he was scared to death.

There was a sharp bend in the riverbank. Kate ran hard, straight to its very edge, and then, without stopping, pushed off against the dirt and stones, diving out as far as she could.

Joey was twenty feet from her when she hit the water.

He was still conscious, but with a wild look in his eyes. He saw Kate and tried to flop his body toward her, his arms flailing at the water. She kicked her feet faster, at the same time yelling to him to float on his back. Though her arms were sore, she kept stroking them through the water.

The current shifted, taking Joey farther to the right, forcing Kate to change direction and cut sharply across toward the other bank. The chop of the river made swimming tough and more than once sent water up her nose. She blew it out as best she could, coughing to clear the water from her throat.

For several anxious seconds, Kate lost sight of him; then Joey's head bobbed up no more than two yards to her left. She yelled and he saw her and stretched an arm out. He was swallowing a lot of water, coughing and choking. She kicked her feet harder, grabbing for his hand, clutching at his outstretched fingers. Their fingertips touched, then slipped away.

Kate kept searching blindly with her hands for him. Fear flooded through her. Where was he? Was he pulled under?

"Don't panic, Joey! Don't panic," she shouted at the empty river.

Taking a deep breath, Kate dove where she had last seen him, almost immediately banging against his shoulder as he fought his way up for air.

As soon as Joey felt her, he grabbed for her, catching

her about the legs. It was just as she remembered from lifesaving class: Someone drowning will twine himself around you like plastic cling wrap out of sheer panic. Kate knew she had to break his hold or he would pull them both down.

Kicking her knees up and banging her hands against his chest loosened his grip, and she broke free. As she turned back toward him, Kate could see Joey's eyes closing. He was slipping into unconsciousness. She grabbed him by his shirt and started swimming toward the riverbank, struggling to keep him from sinking.

The water was no longer rough but she was exhausted, and that made it almost as bad. At times, it was all Kate could do just to hold on to Joey and keep both of them afloat. When she could, she did a sidestroke, and gradually moved them toward the scrubs growing along the edge of the water. She guessed they must have traveled nearly a quarter mile from the rapids before her feet touched bottom and she was able to drag Joey into shallow water.

Pulling him up onto the sand, Kate went over in her mind what she remembered about reviving a near drowner. She turned Joey over onto his stomach and began pushing on his back. She had never tried the technique before except in junior lifesaving. And then it was just practice, no one had drowned, it had all been pretend. So now, with Joey, Kate didn't know if it would work. But after she pushed on his back for less than a minute, water shot out of Joey's mouth and nose, and he began coughing. Almost not believing what was happening, Kate pressed down even harder. A long gasp came from under her.

"What are you doing?" The words came choking out of Joey. Kate jumped from his back and knelt on the ground next to him.

"Are you okay?"

Joey blinked his eyes rapidly, trying to orient himself. Finally, still breathing hard and coughing, he raised his head.

"Yeah, but I feel like I just puked my guts out." He looked around puzzled. "Where's Linda?"

*W*hen Dad and I got back to the apartment, I flopped in the overstuffed chair beside the stereo, and Bear came out of the kitchen wagging his short tail. Bear is a pure black full-size poodle, which means he's as big as a German shepherd. I don't get his hair cut like poodles usually do because I think it looks stupid. Bear has too much dignity to have his hair cut off. Anyway, with his hair long and thick and curly, he looks to me like a bear. So that's his name—Bear.

"And how's my Bear? Did you miss us?" I asked. He stuck his muzzle into my lap, and I scratched him behind his ears, which he really likes. I looked at Dad hanging his jacket on the coat tree.

"Boy, I'm glad that's over with. I like Mrs. Morgan and Linda, but Joey and I won't make it as best buddies. If I never see him again, it will be too soon. Sure am glad I don't have a brother. Boys are nothing but trouble. I feel sorry for Linda, having to live with him and all."

Dad was very quiet. He put his keys on the lamp table where he always keeps them, then sat down in the corner of the couch. He always sits in that spot when he's going to talk to me seriously about something. I said to myself, Here's where I get it. A big lecture on proper manners. He'll most likely send me to an etiquette school to turn me into a proper young lady. The thought of walking primly balancing a book on my head almost made me laugh, but I stifled it and folded my hands.

"I know, Dad. I've got to be more patient with kids. But I was really trying to like him," I said.

"Patient?" Dad asked, looking puzzled. "Oh, you mean with Joe. Well, actually I want to talk to you about something else."

He stopped talking and looked at me. It seemed like minutes and I kept saying to myself, Oh no! Oh no! This is going to be bad. Silence always makes me feel really nervous. I could feel myself getting ready to chew my nails. And I was trying so hard to let them grow long.

His stern-looking face finally broke into a smile. "I'm not mad at you, Kate. I was just thinking about how special you are to me, and how much fun we have together, the two of us."

"It is fun, Dad. You and me. We always have such a good time together." I felt relieved. This wasn't going to be so bad.

Dad's face then changed back to its stern expression. "Kate, I do have to talk to you about something." He stood up with his hands in his pockets and began walking across the room.

"Kate, you know Pamela, uh, Mrs. Morgan, and I

have been dating each other for almost a year. Well we've grown very fond of each other." He stopped beside the television and looked over at me. "The fact is Kate, Pamela and I love each other, and we plan on getting married."

I was stunned. Dad get married. I'd always thought Dad would get married again but not until I was older, maybe when I was twenty-five, not fifteen.

"You're getting married!" I said, not yet believing him.

"I know it's a surprise for you. Pam and I didn't know this would happen, Kate." Dad was walking back and forth across the room now, looking at the floor, gesturing with his hands as he talked. "I always thought you'd be grown up and married before I met someone. But it didn't happen that way. Pam and I can't deny our love for each other, and can't keep going on dating each other twice a week. We need to be with each other. We need to be married, Kate." He stopped beside the stereo and stood watching me.

"I know it means changes in our lives. But you and I, we'll still love each other, we'll still spend time together. And we'll have a family. You'll have a sister and a brother. And though Pam won't replace your mother, she'll be someone for you to talk to about things." He smiled at me again, his eyes full of concern. What he was asking me to do was to feel okay about it, but I didn't. I thought it stank.

"Dad, I'm happy with just you and me. I don't need a sister and a brother. And I don't need Mrs. Morgan to talk to." I could feel my eyes filling up with tears. All of a sudden, everything was changing. Dad could see I was ready to cry and he walked across the room with his long, quick stride. He put his arms around me and held me against his chest. I started to sob.

"Kate, I know it will be hard. I know it's a lot for Pam and me to ask of you kids. But you can't expect Pam and me to stop loving each other."

"I know, Dad. It's just hard to get used to the idea. I haven't had to share you with anyone for a long time."

It's been five years now since Mother left us. As I write this, I can look up and see her picture on the bookshelf. Funny, how if I don't look at it for a while, I have a hard time remembering what she looks like. And when I look at it, it's only occasionally, like now, that I have a twinge of wishing she was with us.

But I don't have the guilt now that I had in the beginning. No gut-tearing feelings that I'm the reason she left. No crying every night, thinking I'm going to crack up. After Dad saw it was eating at me and sat down and talked about it, I've been steadily doing better. I think I believe now what he said about her leaving having nothing to do with me, that it was all him and Mother. But I still sometimes wonder what it was that broke them up, and made her leave. What could be so bad?

Tonight, talking to Dad felt hard again. I found a tissue in my pocket and dabbed at my eyes. "Where would we live? We couldn't all live in this apartment."

Dad rubbed my back, something he's done since I was a little kid whenever I get upset. "Since Pam has such a big house, it makes sense for us to move in with them. You'll have your own room. There'll be plenty of space for all of us, with a big yard for Bear to run around."

"But they live in Brewster. That's a long way. How would I get to school?"

"Kate, it won't be possible for you to continue attending Warren High. You'll have to change schools." He hesitated, the frown marks deepening between his eyebrows. "And it makes more sense if we do it this summer. Then you won't have to change in the middle of a school year."

I couldn't believe what I was hearing. Stop going to Warren. Stop going to school with all my friends.

"No, Dad! That's not fair! I don't want to change schools! I don't want to leave my friends! I want to go to Warren High. Can't I please keep going to Warren? I'm on the swim team and the basketball team!" I pleaded, feeling tears running down my cheeks again. Except for the day Mother left, this was the worst night of my life. I didn't know what I could do to change Dad's mind.

Dad held me by the shoulder. "Kate, I know this is

hard for you. I know you're going to have to make new friends and try out for new teams, but that's the way it'll have to be. Pam and I are getting married next month. We can't afford to live anywhere else but in her house. You will have to accept that! You will have to change schools! I'm sorry."

I pulled away from him and ran to my bedroom. Slamming the door like a little kid, I threw myself onto my bed. "How can you do this to me? How can you make me live with those people?" I sobbed into my pillow.

Later in the night, when I finally fell asleep, I dreamed about my mother. I hadn't dreamed about her in a long time. The dream was all mixed up and confusing, but one part was real clear. She was yelling at Dad while putting everything she could into a gigantic suitcase. Really weird. Clothes, shoes, toaster oven, curtains, rugs, the couch, the washing machine, everything you could think of went into the suitcase. And then she tried to put me in as well, but I was too big. There simply wasn't enough room. She kept trying every which way possible to put me inside the suitcase, but I just wouldn't fit. Finally, she just dropped me onto the floor and left. She wouldn't take even one thing out of the suitcase to fit me in. No, she took the junk and left me.

Talk about being upset. In the dream, I sat on the floor where she'd dropped me and cried like a baby, cried that my mother was leaving me. But instead of making crying noises, I whined and howled. The howling part was so awful, so upsetting in my dream, that I woke up shaking. At first, I wasn't sure where I was, especially since I still heard the howling. Was it really coming from me? And then, lying in my bed, in the darkness, pulling the covers about me for comfort, I heard Dad yelling at Bear to stop it.

Of course, it was Bear. He was lying outside my closed door where he always sleeps when he can't get into my room. And he'd heard something, some noise far away that no human could hear. And he howled to let us know that he didn't like whatever he was hearing.

When Bear howls he sounds almost like a wolf, giving me the shivers up and down my spine. But last night, Bear's howling made me shiver worse than ever. I shook and shook and shook under the bedcovers. Well, maybe it wasn't really so much Bear's howling, as it was dreaming about my mother leaving me. And maybe feeling that my dad is now also leaving me.

The Oskeet River:

11:14 A.M., THURSDAY, JULY 12

Kate hurried along the bank, looking for Linda, for any sign of her yellow top in the water, on the rocks, or along the edge of the river. Joey followed a few yards behind her, stumbling at times over roots and stones, breathing hard from his near-drowning.

They reached the worst of the rapids. The spray was so heavy, drenching them like a downpour, that Kate had to shield her eyes to see. The gray shapes of the rocks were all that could be made out through the sheets of water thrown high into the air. If Linda was among those rocks, Kate knew she and Joey would never find her, and that Linda would drown for sure. The thought that maybe Linda had already drowned troubled Kate, but she refused to let herself believe it. She pushed the thought out of her head by quickening her pace along the riverbank.

When they reached the beginning of the rapids, the spray was much finer. Kate could see better but still there was no sign of Linda. Together, the two of them scanned every rock and log but there was nothing.

Kate was about to turn back the other way when Joey grabbed her arm. "What's that?"

Kate looked across the river to where he was pointing on the other side. She could definitely see something over there, something caught between two logs, something yellow. But is it big enough to be Linda? Kate asked herself. Could Linda have gotten all the way to the other side? It didn't make sense, not with the current pulling so hard in the opposite direction.

Kate couldn't make it out. Whatever it was, it wasn't moving. It just lay there among the logs. If it wasn't Linda, and she swam across to find out, she would have wasted a lot of time. It might then be too late to find Linda alive. She didn't know what to do. Shielding her eyes from the sun, Kate strained to see across the river, as if she could make the yellow thing, whatever it was, move by staring at it.

"Linda! Linda!" Kate yelled as loud as she could across the river, praying the yellow she saw was Linda. Just let her hear me and move an arm or something, she said to herself. But she or it didn't move.

"Joey, do you think it's Linda?"

"I don't know. It's so far away." He was standing on a rock. His shirt was off, pressed against the cut on his cheek.

"I have to find out." Kate heard herself saying the words even before she was sure she was going. "I can't take the chance that it isn't. I'm going to swim across. Why don't you walk back down the bank and keep looking for Linda. If you see her, wave your shirt over your head. I'll look for you every few minutes to see if you've found her. If I find her, I'll wave to you, okay?"

"Sure, but how are you going to get across? You'll crash into the rocks."

Kate looked at the fast-moving current. "I'll have to go farther up, where the water is slower." She forced herself to smile to hide the jitters she was feeling. She didn't like the idea of swimming across the river. She had had her fill of swimming for the day. Besides feeling tired, her fear that Linda might have drowned was making a tight knot in her stomach.

"Listen," Kate said. "If anything happens to me, remember that to get back to camp you just follow the river the way we came."

Surprise and then what seemed like worry crossed Joey's face, as if it hadn't occurred to him that he might be left alone. For an instant, tears glistened in his eyes, but he fought them off by biting his lip.

"Nothing's going to happen to you, giraffe breath," he said, then turned away abruptly and started back down the bank, pushing his way through the scrub pines.

Kate watched him for a few seconds, wondering what was going on inside his head. Then, turning away herself, she hurried upriver.

After a quarter mile Kate stopped at a wide bend in the bank. The water was flowing much slower at this point, not giving a clue of the rocks that lay ahead. She glanced back along the edge of the river, looking for Joey, but he was nowhere in sight.

Finding a spot a few feet out from the bank where the water was free of logs and deep enough, Kate dove in. Instantly, tears filled her eyes as the river stung the small cuts on her face and hands. She took a deep breath, and forcing herself to ignore the stinging, started stroking through the water as quickly as she could.

Though Kate was a good swimmer, she was more tired than she realized. Her strokes became steadily slower until the last fifty feet felt like she was swimming through molasses.

Finally, her heart racing, Kate collapsed on the riverbank. She lay on her side, her chest rising and falling with short, rapid breaths. When enough of her strength returned, Kate raised her head and looked back across the river for a sign of Joey. But the thick spray from the rapids made it hard to see anything on the other side.

Kate pushed herself up from the wet sand and tried to tell where she had seen what she desperately wanted to be Linda. Having come downriver farther than she had planned, she knew she had to be fairly close.

Five large rocks lay between her and the beginning of the worst part of the rapids. If Linda was on this side of the river, Kate knew she had to be somewhere among them.

Kate was almost to the third rock when through the churning water she glimpsed yellow. Running as quickly as she could toward it, she knew somehow that it wouldn't be Linda. Just the same, her heart sank when she saw among rotting logs a deflated, yellow life jacket.

Kate was now really scared for Linda. She looked for Joey and this time saw him directly across the river from her. Though he seemed to see her too, he wasn't waving his shirt, which could only mean he hadn't found Linda either.

Feeling too weak to cross back to Joey, Kate was forced to search this side of the river. She knew that with every passing minute the chance of finding Linda alive got smaller.

Kate hurried along the riverbank, her eyes searching back and forth across the water and between the rocks. The rapids didn't kick up as much spray along this stretch, so she could see better. She was almost past the last of the boulders when something caught her eye, something wedged between two smaller rocks. Not bright yellow, but more a dirty yellow. Was it another life jacket? As Kate ran toward it, her breath caught in her throat. Linda.

From Kate Evans's Diary:

SATURDAY, MAY 12

*T*he Brewster Shopping Mall wasn't exactly my first choice for where I wanted to be on a Saturday afternoon. But today, there I was with Linda Morgan, us trying to walk together and still get through the crowds of shoppers.

Dad and Mrs. Morgan had decided this morning, through some kind of weird adult thinking, that Linda and I should spend the afternoon getting to know each other better by shopping for dresses for the wedding.

The wedding, their wedding, has become the main event in their lives. As Dad and Mrs. Morgan get more excited, I'm sinking lower and lower. The wedding will be the beginning of all that I dread, and it's set to happen in three weeks.

"So, where do you think we should look first?" Linda asked me.

"Look? Oh, the dresses." For a second there in the mall, thinking about the wedding, I had forgotten what we were supposed to be doing.

Looking at Linda and trying to think about dresses, I realized just how pretty she is. Her long, blond hair was pulled up high on her head in a ponytail. My own short hair was straggly in comparison, with brittle ends from the chlorine of all the swimming pools I've been in this year. In my sweatshirt and jeans, I just knew I looked the country hick. While Linda, in her bright white sneaks, white skirt, and pink top, looked like the cute cheerleader she is. We were a pair, as opposite as you could get.

Thinking that maybe, just maybe, I wouldn't look so ugly if Linda's prettiness wasn't right up against me for everyone to see the contrast, I moved off to the side, letting a fat woman with a kid in a stroller get between us. From now on, I said to myself, this is how I'm going to have to go through life, always keeping a fat person between me and Linda. What a fun life it's going to be.

Peering around the woman at Linda, I said, "Sure is crowded. Listen, I don't know this mall. Why don't you pick a store to go to?"

She smiled. "Okay. There's a store just up ahead that usually has nice dresses. We can try there."

The Deb Shop was ablaze with scribbles of neon lights across its front making it for sure the brightest store in the mall. You felt like you should be wearing shades just to go near it. And the displays of clothes hanging at all sorts of angles up and down the walls were so wild and colorful—pinks and yellows and purples and turquoises—that it looked at first like some kind of weird nightclub.

It was the kind of store to attract high school kids who were with-it, or wanted to think they were with-it. And wouldn't you know, as soon as we walked into the place this girl with her boyfriend tagging along behind spotted Linda. Yelling across the racks of clothes, she pushed her way toward us through the dresses.

The girl was a slightly taller and not as pretty copy of Linda. She had long blond hair pulled into a pony-tail at the side of her head, purplish blush marks across her cheekbones, matching lipstick, and blue eye-shadow. But what you really noticed were her big boobs pushing out her skintight sweater.

Her boyfriend was maybe an inch or two taller than I, and dressed in jeans and a Penn State sweatshirt. Okay clothes, but not exactly a brand name wardrobe. He was no Tom Cruise but he was okay looking and had a cute smile. The smile seemed to be stuck to his face as if he was nervous.

Seeing them coming, knowing I was the outsider, and not wanting to feel awkward, I slid off between the racks of clothes, pretending to look for a dress. But there were soon signs my strategy wasn't working. I could see the three of them talking and glancing over at me, especially the boyfriend, who was stand-ing closest to Linda. Sure enough Linda called me over.

"Kate, I'd like you to meet Jennifer and Bob. They

go to Brewster High with me. Kate is, uh, a friend of mine." Her face reddened, letting me know she didn't know how to introduce me. What should she say— "This is my future stepsister"?

"Linda said you live in Warren," the girl, Jennifer, said, looking me up and down, her purple Halloween lips frowning. No hello, no smile. "Don't they have clothing stores there?"

"Knock it off, Jen!" It was the nervous boyfriend suddenly not seeming so nervous. With his hands on his girlfriend's arms, he pulled her firmly off to the side.

"Don't mind Jen, she's like that with everyone." He had such a warm smile I couldn't help but like him.

"Linda said you might be switching to Brewster High." He was being very friendly, absolutely ignoring his girlfriend's angry looks.

I hesitated, not wanting to admit the possibility; but having to say something, I finally said, "Maybe in September."

He nodded, still smiling. I noticed he had bright blue eyes. "Okay, well I hope I see you. I'll look for you in the halls." By now his girlfriend was pulling at his arm. "Jeez, Jen, okay! But I thought you wanted to look around this store." He was quickly pulled away, waving a hand at us.

Linda came up to me laughing. "Sorry about that. Jennifer's a bit of a snob."

I started laughing too. "Guess I won't be able to count her as a close friend."

"No way, not when you almost stole her boyfriend from her."

"What are you saying? Do you think he liked me?" The thought that a boy would be attracted to me was a real shocker.

"Of course. Didn't you see how nervous he was? He's not usually nervous like that. It was Bob who wanted to meet you, not Jennifer. And when she realized he was interested in you, that's when she got all snooty. Didn't you see him eyeing you?"

"No." This was blowing me away. "Linda, before we look at dresses, how about we get a soda. I'm feeling thirsty all of a sudden."

We sat in a booth in the Burger King sipping our Pepsis. "He's kind of cute, isn't he?"

"Who? Bob? Do you like him?" She was smiling at me over her drink.

I felt embarrassed and almost didn't answer. "No boy has ever been interested in me before."

"Come on! That can't be true! You're so pretty!"

"Pretty! Me! I look like a giraffe! I so wish I was smaller like you and had long hair, not this bird's nest." I pushed my hand through my hair. "I look like a country hick!"

Linda looked straight at me without smiling. "I think

you're very pretty. You have a long, elegant figure and a clear complexion, and when they take off your braces, you'll have a beautiful smile. You may want to be smaller, but I'd like to be taller. And don't you know that your body's still developing? Why, in another year I bet you have the figure of a model. And all models are tall, you know that. Kate, I'm envious of you!"

I couldn't take all this in. In half an hour, my whole idea of myself had gotten turned upside down. And at the same time I was seeing Linda very differently too. She didn't seem to be against me like I thought she'd be. When I talked to her, she listened like a friend.

"Are you always so direct, and so . . . well, supportive?" I asked.

Linda frowned. "Sorry, I guess I say what I think. Mom tells me I should be more tactful. She's right. People don't always like it when I'm honest with them. But sometimes, like now, I just . . ." She didn't finish. She looked down at her drink.

"Linda, I'm one person who likes listening to you, especially when you're boosting my ego." That got a smile from her. On a wild impulse I said to her, "Now here's something I'd really like to hear what you think about. How do you feel about our parents getting married?"

Her eyes looked up at me as if startled. "That's a blockbuster question."

"Yeah, but I'd really like to know what you think."

She was quiet for a moment, sipping at her Pepsi; then unexpectedly, from the corners of her eyes tears dripped onto her cheeks. I was surprised.

"Honest?" she asked. And I nodded.

"I don't know for sure, Kate." She wiped at her eyes with a napkin. "I want my mom to be happy, and she says that your dad makes her happy, that they love each other." She shrugged her shoulders. "So, I guess it's good that it's happening. But sometimes I miss my dad and wish he hadn't died. And I guess I wonder how things will change when you and your dad move in, and if that will be bad. And I get a little scared." She twirled her straw in her soda and was quiet for a couple of seconds, then looked at me. "How do you feel about it?"

"At first, I felt angry, angry about having to change schools and leave my friends. But then, when I knew it was definitely going to happen, I started feeling scared, scared I'll be left out of things. And not fit in. And scared my dad won't have time to do things with me, like swim and canoe." It was so easy to talk to Linda, all the things I hadn't told anyone just came out. Finally, I stopped. There was nothing else to say.

We sat quietly, finishing our drinks, just kind of feeling things.

After a while, Linda put her drink cup down on the table and looked at me with a small smile. "Thanks for asking me how I felt. Us talking about this stuff really helps. It all doesn't seem so strange when I know you feel some of the things I do."

"Yeah, I think I feel better too." I really did. I felt more comfortable with Linda. So maybe she isn't a super close friend, not yet anyway, but neither is she someone who's going to treat me rotten. "Jeez, look at the time!" I said. "We better get going! It'll take ages to find a dress for my . . . elegant figure." Linda laughed.

The Oskeet River:

11:36 A.M., THURSDAY, JULY 12

Linda was lying on her side, wedged between two rocks, the river surging around her. She lay so still, the thought of her being dead sent chills through Kate.

Joey had kept up with Kate along the other side of the river so he was directly across from her. She climbed quickly onto a tree stump and waved her arms over her head until he saw her and waved back. She could tell by how he jumped around that he was excited, but her own excitement was gone.

Her stomach kept turning over as she waded out toward Linda. Kate tried not to think that Linda might be dead, tried not to think that her blond head might be cracked open on the rock.

"Linda are you okay?" Kate yelled as loud as she could, trying for Linda to hear her over the roar of the rapids, but she could barely hear herself. She felt she was yelling into a thunderstorm. She pushed through the water as fast as she could, trying to keep her footing in the strong current, her heart galloping. She was scared to death for Linda.

Kate reached the rocks and raised Linda's head carefully, wiping the spray off her face, looking for any bleeding. Linda's eyelids flickered. She was alive.

"Linda," Kate said loudly. "Can you hear me? Are you hurt?"

Though open, Linda's eyes looked blankly at Kate, as if not recognizing her. Kate started to ask again if she was hurt, when Linda's lips moved like she was trying to speak. Kate bent closer and listened. But all she heard was the roaring of the river around them.

"What did you say?" Kate yelled. But Linda's eyes had already closed.

Kate knew she had to get Linda out of the water. Even if she was seriously hurt, Kate couldn't leave her between the rocks. She didn't know how long it might be before help came. It might be days. Pamela and her father didn't know they had canoed down this part of the river. The two were sure to search the north branch of the Oskeet first.

Climbing around behind the rocks made it easier for Kate to get hold of Linda. She caught her under her armpits and with some pulling lifted her out from between the rocks. Though Linda wasn't a big girl, she was dead weight, making her hard to move.

Kate pulled Linda through the water, walking slowly to keep her footing on the stony bottom. Because of the rapids, the current was strong, and felt even stronger with Linda's weight on her.

Though Kate had only twenty feet of water to fight through, those twenty feet felt to her like a hundred. And when she finally reached the riverbank, it took all her remaining strength to lift Linda up onto it.

Kate collapsed beside Linda, her chest heaving. She felt exhausted. There wasn't a day she could remember working so hard, not even during swim team training. Breathing through her mouth, she sat up and stretched Linda out on her back.

Large bruises blotched Linda'a arms and legs, and her hands and face were covered with cuts. But she was breathing, and that was what mattered. Kate began slowly checking Linda's body, looking for something else, anything that might tell her if Linda was hurt worse.

Remembering that one of Linda's legs had looked odd when she was lifting her out of the water, Kate held them together. The cockeyed angle of Linda's right leg was now obvious, and could only mean a break.

Kate moved the leg carefully. She didn't want to force it, but she needed to know how bad it was. Gently sliding her hands down the leg, she thought that it was broken in at least two places. A compound fracture, Kate knew, was bad. Luckily, the ends of the bones hadn't torn through the skin.

As she moved the broken leg into what she hoped was a more comfortable position, Kate heard Linda moan. She turned quickly toward her, anxious, wanting her to be awake. But Linda's eyes were still closed, the blond eyelashes barely visible on her pale face.

It was the pain from the broken leg, Kate realized.

The pain had to be terrible for her to moan while unconscious. Kate prayed it was just the leg and not anything worse. A broken leg was bad enough. She didn't know what she would do if Linda was bleeding inside her brain or somewhere else.

Linda's leg had to be splinted. The first aid course Kate had taken at the Red Cross had taught her that. But to do it she needed help. Splinting Linda's leg had to be done carefully so as not to damage the leg more. As little as Kate liked the idea, Joey was the only one who could help her. And he was across the river. How am I going to get him over here? she asked herself.

Kate looked toward the rocks where she had seen him last. There was no sign of him. As the spray from the rapids was fairly thick, she went down along the bank a short way, but still couldn't see him. Where has he gone? she wondered. She didn't want to think that he might be trying to swim across the river by himself. He had proved to her once already just how awful a swimmer he was. If that was what he was doing, she was sure he would drown.

She had to find him. After an anxious glance back at Linda, Kate ran along the bank, looking across to the far side for any sign of Joey. Finally, up ahead of her, a quarter mile away, where the river bent to the left, she saw an orange dot on the water. The uneasy feeling in her stomach told her it was Joey. As she ran down the riverbank, she could see him better. He had found one of their life jackets, tied it around himself, and was now swimming across the river with it.

He was two-thirds of the way across, kicking madly with his feet, and beating the water with his arms like he was punching a pillow. Kate admitted to herself that he was a brave kid—stupid, but brave.

She reached the bend in the river when he was still fifteen feet from the bank. He looked worn out, his arms hanging limp in the water.

"Is Linda okay?" he yelled.

Kate shook her head. "No, she's got a badly broken leg." She waded into the water and caught his arm. "You're an idiot to cross the river by yourself, but I'm glad you're here. I need your help. Linda's—"

"I couldn't stay over there, Kate," he interrupted. "I had to come across. Jeez, I thought maybe she was dead, a broken leg doesn't sound so bad."

Kate pulled him to his feet. "The broken leg is all I can see, but she's also unconscious. I hope it's just from the pain, but I don't know. We have to get her to a doctor."

"Unconscious!" The excitement drained from Joey's face. "Where is she?"

"Back by the rapids. Come on!"

When they reached Linda, Kate was glad to see her still lying in the same position. But her leg looked worse. Out of the cool water, it was starting to swell.

"Joey, we have to make a splint. Let's see if we can

find some branches. We can tie them around her leg with the straps from that life jacket you have."

"Is she going to die, Kate?"

Joey's question hit Kate unexpectedly. She turned to look at him. He was kneeling on the ground beside his sister. Seeing him wiping tears from his eyes, knowing how scared he was, Kate couldn't tell him that the possibility of Linda dying scared her as well.

"No, she's not going to die. But we've got to get her to a doctor," Kate answered him quietly. She hoped the future would prove her right.

From Kate Evans's Diary:
SATURDAY, JUNE 2

*T*his morning, Linda and I were in her bedroom dressing for the wedding. It's a pretty room decorated in pastel greens. There's a canopy over her bed with a butterfly pattern that matches her curtains and bedspread. And on her walls, she has framed needlepoints her grandmother did for her, and posters of Ireland where she says she wants to go some day.

"Will you zip me up, Kate?" Linda asked, turning so the back of her dress was toward me.

Dad and Mrs. Morgan changed their minds and decided to get married in the backyard of the house. They thought it would be romantic. Personally, for romance I'd pick Paris. The French are so . . . so . . . well they're French. But not a backyard in Brewster.

"How do I look?" Linda asked, modeling her new dress, making a ballet pirouette so that the dress swirled around her. It was a soft yellow color with a touch of lace.

"You look very pretty," I said. And she did. Her long blond hair was thick and luxuriant, hanging down to the middle of her back.

"And how does my elegant figure look?" I asked, standing up in my new cream and powder blue dress, wobbling nervously in my first high heels. I knew Linda would give me her most honest opinion.

She walked around me, looking me up and down, her hand on her chin as if she were judging a horse. Her eyes were so serious, I knew for sure the dress was too short or the color didn't suit me.

Seeing me ready to collapse into a jittery mess, she laughed. "The only thing I can find wrong is a lack of confidence in the girl inside the dress. You look lovely, Kate. You do, I mean it."

I felt thrilled. Dad always tells me I'm pretty, but dads are prejudiced. Having another girl, a girl whose opinion I'm getting to respect, tell me the same thing makes a big difference.

I laughed with her. Linda and I are still unsure of how we're suppose to act with each other, and still scared about how things are going to work out with all of us in the same house. But we don't feel like strangers with each other anymore.

I can't say that about me and Joey. He's hardly ever around when I am, and when he is, he seems to be avoiding me. Not just me, he's also avoiding Dad. For a kid that's going to be my stepbrother, I don't know much about him. His name, his age, and that he can be a brat is about it.

"We sure lucked out on these dresses. Can you believe they were both thirty percent off?" Linda asked, admiring herself in the mirror over the bureau.

"It was really wild, especially when they're so pretty.

Got to admit, in these dresses we're two foxy ladies," I said. We both broke up laughing.

A quick knock on the door made us both turn. Mrs. Morgan, her face flushed, came hurrying into the room.

"Oh, that boy! I don't know what I'm going to do with him." Seeing us in our dresses, she stopped and smiled. "I'm sorry girls. You both look so pretty. I didn't mean to burst in on you when you're getting ready."

She hadn't changed her clothes. She was still wearing the blouse and jeans she was wearing when Dad and I arrived this morning for breakfast. She had two curlers in her hair and no makeup on and the wedding was supposed to happen in less than an hour.

"Mom, why aren't you dressed?" Linda asked, surprised. "Don't you know what time it is?" She turned to look at the clock on her dresser. "Look! It's almost ten-thirty."

"Linda, I know. I've been looking for Joey and I can't find him. He's not in his room. He's not in the house. The new suit he was going to wear is still hanging in his closet. Where is he? Why is he doing this?" Her upper lip was trembling. She looked like she was ready to cry.

Linda put her arm around her mother. "Mom, everything will be okay. Don't cry." She looked at me. "Kate and I will find him. You go and get dressed. I think I know where he might be."

"Where?"

"In the garage."

Mrs. Morgan sniffed and wiped her eyes with her fingers. "Yes, of course. That's where he most likely is. I forgot. But I think you and I should go." She turned to me. "Kate, would you tell your dad we'll just be a few minutes. That we've gone to get Joey, that he needs some"—she hesitated—"some attention." She smiled weakly.

I nodded, not really sure I knew what was happening, and watched them hurry out of the room. The feeling of being a stranger here hit me again. Who are these people I'm going to be living with? The three of them are a family that I'll never be a part of. Will Dad? Will he become part of their family and leave me behind? Suddenly, I feel very afraid, and very lonely, the same afraidness and loneliness I felt when Mother left.

The Oskeet River:

12:36 P.M., THURSDAY, JULY 12

*W*ill these work? Are these okay for the splint?"

Kate looked at the sticks Joey was holding. "They might be too long. Why don't you measure them against Linda's leg, and break off what we don't need?"

As Joey measured and broke the sticks, Kate ripped the nylon straps off the two life jackets they had found. The straps were all she could think to use to tie the sticks together into a splint.

With the straps and sticks beside her on the ground, Kate carefully straightened Linda's leg as far as she could without making it worse. The leg looked terribly swollen. And every time she touched it, Linda moaned.

Kate hated seeing Linda hurting. And it worried her that Linda was still unconscious. If she had banged her head on a rock and suffered a concussion, Kate didn't know what to do.

Looking at Linda lying on the ground, Kate remembered how whenever she was sick her dad would put a cool washcloth on her forehead. It always helped her feel better. Maybe it would help Linda. Kate tore a piece off the bottom of Linda's wet shirt and gently placed it on Linda's forehead. Kate didn't know what else to do.

With Joey helping to keep the leg still, Kate bound the branches along Linda's thigh and calf. She tried to remember the picture in the first aid book she had at home. The splint didn't look as good as the drawing in the book but she thought it might work.

But a splint wasn't enough; if they were going to get Linda back to camp, they would have to carry her. It was the only way. That meant they would have to make a stretcher.

But first, the cloth on Linda's forehead needed to be wetter and colder if it was going to do any good. Kate took the cloth and walked down to the edge of the river.

A strong breeze was starting to blow along the water, bending the pine trees back away from the riverbank. Looking up, she saw large, dark clouds sweeping in from the west, the direction of the mountains. Kate had been camping long enough with her father to know the signs of a coming storm, and this one looked like it might be a bad one.

Soaking the cloth, Kate yelled up the bank to Joey. "A storm's coming. We better make a stretcher pretty fast. See if you can find a couple of strong tree branches we can use for poles."

She could see Joey sitting on the ground beside Linda. He felt scared for his sister. And why shouldn't he? Kate asked herself. He loves Linda. In saying that, Kate felt strangely envious. She knew her dad loved her, but did anyone else? Her mother? Her mother never wrote anymore to tell her.

"Kate, Linda's eyes are open! She's awake!" Joey shouted excitedly.

Kate ran up the bank as fast as she could, the wet cloth clenched in her hand. Linda's face was still pale, but her eyes were finally open. Kate knelt down across from Joey.

"Linda can you hear me?"

Linda looked at them and smiled weakly. "Sure. Oh, jeez!" She winced. "My leg hurts something awful!"

"Try not to move! You busted your leg." Joey's usually loud voice was almost a whisper. "Kate and I put a splint on it."

"That's right. You got banged up on the rocks. Try to lie still. We're going to make a stretcher to carry you." Kate smiled at her as reassuringly as she could. "Maybe this will help you feel better." She put the wet cloth across Linda's forehead. "You were unconscious a long time. We were getting worried. Do you think you hit your head?"

"I don't know." Linda reached up and touched her hair. "I remember flipping over in the water and trying to get to the surface. I have never been so scared." She squeezed her eyes shut. "Oh, God! My leg hurts really bad! I don't know if I can stand it!"

Kate looked helplessly at Joey. What could they do? They didn't even have aspirin. The first aid kit was back at camp. She felt Linda's fingers tighten around hers.

"Linda, we don't have anything to give you." Tears filled Kate's eyes as she watched Linda's face scrunch up from the pain. They had to do something. But what?

Kate's fingers were going numb from Linda squeezing them so hard, but the squeezing seemed to help her. That gave Kate an idea. She searched the ground for a small stick. When she found one, she wiped off the dirt and peeled away the bark.

"Linda, when the pain is bad, bite down on this stick. You know like in the movies when cowboys get arrows cut out of them, and they bite down on bullets." She felt next to useless giving it to her, but the stick was all Kate could think of.

She watched Linda put it between her teeth and bite down. Linda bit so deep into the wood, Kate knew the pain had to be excruciating. They had to get Linda to a doctor as fast as they could. Kate tapped Joey on the arm.

"Come on. We have to make that stretcher."

After some looking, Kate found two tree branches lying in the tall grass, victims of a past storm. The branches were nearly as thick as her arm, and looked strong. After breaking off the twigs that grew out of them like porcupine quills, Kate was glad to see that the branches were straighter than she first thought.

They now had two poles for the stretcher, but what were they going to string between them for Linda to lie on? The two life jackets were the only things Kate could think of. Somehow, they would have to make them work.

Kate stretched the life jackets between the poles and stood back to look at them. Though the arm holes made big gaps, she thought there was still enough nylon cloth and rubber to support Linda. The only problem she could see was how to tie the life jackets to the poles. She felt dumb not having thought about how to make the stretcher before making the splint.

"Ripping the straps off was really stupid," she said, turning to Joey. "They would have been perfect for tying the jackets to the poles. We could have found something else for the splint. What are we going to use to tie them together?"

Joey stood up. "You're right, it was stupid! The straps would have worked great. You always make things worse, don't you."

His anger surprised Kate. They were stuck out in the middle of nowhere with Linda badly hurt, and he was starting another fight with her. I'm doing my best. Why does he always put me down?

"Since you messed things up, guess I have to fix it," he said. He turned away and walked toward the bushes growing along the riverbank, looking all around him.

Kate felt hurt and angry. Does he think he can do

better? How is he going to fix it? Does he think he's going to find rope just lying on the ground out here?

"Hey, Kate! Maybe we can use this!"

Angry that Joey thought everything was so easy to fix, that he thought he could do better, Kate walked over to where he was pulling at a bush, ready to yell at him.

"This vine is pretty tough, almost like rope. Look!" He tugged on the pencil-thick, woody stem. "See! I can't break it! These vines are growing all through the bushes along here. Maybe we can use them. We could wrap them around the poles and through the holes in the life jackets enough times, and tie them tight enough that they'll hold and won't break."

"Don't be silly! Vines won't hold Linda's weight. Just because you can't break them doesn't mean they won't break. Look, let me show you."

Not sure she was right, but determined to show Joey that he wasn't so hot himself, Kate wrapped her hands tightly around one of the vines and pulled. It didn't break. Her face reddened. She wasn't going to let this brat show her up. She jerked harder, lost her balance, and fell with the vine loose in her hand. She had jerked it right out of the ground.

"See, I know some things too. You don't know everything." Joey turned away, unsmiling, and started tugging a vine out of one of the bushes.

Okay, Kate, you got to admit that maybe he's right,

Kate said to herself. Maybe we can use the vines. It's worth trying. What else can we do? And is it so bad that he thought of it? She took a deep breath and sighed.

Putting her hand on Joey's arm, she said, "Joey, I'm sorry if I hurt your feelings by not believing you."

"Don't worry. I'm too dumb to get my feelings hurt." Without looking at Kate, he jerked his arm away and walked over to the next bush.

Kate found another vine rooted in the ground and jerked at it until it popped out. Why do I have such a big mouth? I always say the wrong thing. After knocking the dirt off its stringy roots, Kate carried the vine back to where they had left Linda and began wrapping it around one of the stretcher poles, through the holes in the life jackets, pulling the jackets tight against the pole, tying knots everywhere she could. She knew she and Joey had to work together. No good would come of them fighting, not now.

Joey finally came back with the vines he'd found and began working on the other side of the stretcher. He didn't look at Kate and didn't say anything. He just knelt on the ground, looking angry, his hands pulling and tugging to make sure the vines were as tight as possible.

They wrapped the vines around and around the poles until it was hard to see the bark in places. When they finished, to try the stretcher out, Kate lay down on the life jackets and Joey lifted first one end then the other. It wasn't what she would call comfortable but it felt strong enough to carry Linda. The poles bent but not too much.

They placed the stretcher on the ground up against Linda. Then, stroking her long, blond hair, now wet and matted from the river, Kate talked to her as re-assuringly as she could.

"Linda, we're going to lift you onto the stretcher. I know your leg'll hurt. But we'll try to be as gentle as we can." Linda smiled slightly and pointed to the stick she was still clenching between her teeth.

Kneeling on opposite sides of Linda, Kate and Joey snaked their arms underneath her. When she saw that Joey had his arms under Linda's back and she felt the splinted leg resting on her own arms, Kate took a deep breath.

"Ready! Lift!"

Linda helped them by pushing her hands against the ground. Watching her face scrunch up from the pain, her teeth digging into the stick, Kate kept thinking how brave her new sister was.

Then Linda was up on the stretcher, lying very still, and suddenly Kate was frightened. Horrible thoughts filled her head that maybe they weren't strong enough to carry Linda all the way back to camp. And what would happen if they weren't? Would Linda die? In that moment, Kate felt so scared she started trembling.

Kate wanted Linda to be safe. She wanted them all to be safe. She closed her eyes tightly for a moment to still her shaking. We'll get her back! We'll get her back! she said over and over to herself, thinking positively like her dad always told her to do. Gradually, she felt less frightened, and she knew that she would try her best. She just hoped her best would be good enough.

Seeing Linda watching her, Kate smiled self-consciously.

"We're going to start now. We'll be careful, I promise." Linda smiled back.

Kate looked at Joey. The worry and fear she felt were reflected in his face. He no longer looked angry.

"I'll lead the way," she said as matter-of-factly as she could.

Checking Linda one more time, Kate saw her clench her hands into fists, as if knowing more pain was coming. Swallowing hard, Kate crouched down and grasped the ends of the poles. Looking over her shoulder, she saw that Joey was ready.

"Okay, let's lift," Kate said quietly. Pushing with their leg muscles, they stood up. With Linda on it, the makeshift stretcher creaked and bent between them, but it held her.

Linda didn't feel too heavy to Kate, but she had an idea it wouldn't be long before her arms would get tired and it would start feeling like Linda weighed a ton.

Kate looked back at Joey again. "I'm okay," he said, sounding almost surprised.

"Let's go then. We'll walk as fast as we can but not so fast that we fall. If you get tired, yell."

They started, and Kate quickly found out they wouldn't be walking fast, not with the stretcher. It was too awkward. Every step she took, the stretcher hit her in the back of the legs. She tried holding the poles a little behind her, and that helped even if it strained her shoulders more.

They had a long way to go. If she was right, Kate figured they had canoed almost ten miles. She hoped they could do a mile an hour. At that speed, it was going to take them ten hours to get back to camp. That didn't allow for resting, but did allow for a lot of luck. Kate could only hope they'd have that luck.

The three of them were in terrible trouble. They were miles from camp, Linda needed a doctor desperately, and they didn't have any food. Kate had thought the day she and her dad moved into the house with Joey and Linda and their mom had been bad, but it was nothing like this.

From Kate Evans's Diary:
F R I D A Y ,   J U N E   1 5

*T*his afternoon, I began moving into the Morgan house. I stood in the doorway, looking into my new bedroom with Mrs. Morgan—now I guess she's Mrs. Evans—smiling brightly at me. I didn't know what to call her. Calling her "Mother" didn't feel right, and calling her Pamela sounded disrespectful. So I avoided calling her anything.

"Kate, this is your room. It needs to be fixed up and painted. But I thought you would want to do that. Tomorrow, we can go to the paint store and pick out some paint."

The room is smaller than my bedroom at the apartment. The windows are tiny, the walls are a gloomy green, and this afternoon, there were boxes piled in a jumble in one corner. If you want to be depressed the room is perfect.

"Maybe you could paint it a bright sunshine yellow and hang a lot of cheerful posters. And we could get a new carpet. What do you think?" Mrs. Morgan asked eagerly. I found it hard to share her enthusiasm but I had to say something.

"That sounds great. But I think I'd prefer lavender

or maybe raspberry," I said and walked into the room. "I'll put my bed against this wall and my bureau over here." I pointed to the wall opposite the windows.

"Kate, are these your boxes?" I turned around. Mrs. Morgan was opening one of the boxes in the corner. "No, I can see they're Joey's. Oh, that boy! I told him to get all his things out of here. He was using this room to store his junk."

She walked quickly out into the hall and called loudly. "Joey! Joey! Come into the extra—I mean come into Kate's bedroom right now!" When she heard him coming, she came back into the room.

"Mrs. Morgan if—" Jeez, it came out. I felt like an idiot. Even if I was thinking it, how could I let myself actually call her Mrs. Morgan when she was now married to Dad.

"Kate, it's okay. It must be hard to call me 'Mother' or 'Mom.' You haven't known me very long, and you're nearly grown up yourself. Why don't you call me Pamela? At least, it's not so formal," she said smiling.

"I don't know. Calling you by your first name just doesn't seem right." I hesitated. "But maybe it's better than Mrs. Morgan, I mean Mrs. Evans."

"Fine. Then it's settled. You'll call me Pamela, and I'll call you Kate. Now, where is that boy?" She went to the door and called for him.

"Pamela," I said her name quickly, self-consciously. Saying it sounded strange and impolite. "If these are

Joey's boxes, they can stay here awhile. I won't get all my stuff moved in till tomorrow anyway." I didn't want Joey to get yelled at. Dad would be angry if I caused trouble my first day in the house. I really wanted to be friends with everyone, including Joey.

"No, I told him to move everything out before you came." Joey slouched into the room in a red T-shirt and flowered shorts. When he saw me he raised the corners of his lips in a fake smile.

"Joey, I told you two days ago to move these boxes out of here. Kate is moving her things in. Now, get them out!"

"But Mom, where can I put them? There's no space in my room."

"You can put them in the attic or throw them out. I don't care! But if the boxes are not out of here by lunchtime, they'll go straight to the trash! You've got too much junk, that's the problem." Her cheeks were flushed with anger. "Kate, I'll be back in a minute. I have something downstairs for you." She walked quickly out of the room.

I was left with Joey, who was bent over two large boxes, trying to lift them off the floor. I went to him and put my hands on the top box. "Let me help you."

He dropped the boxes and stood up, brushing my arm away. "I don't need your help. I can do it by myself."

"What are you so mad about? I'm just trying to help you."

"You want to help?" He looked toward the door, then back at me. "You want to help? Then go away! Get out of my face!"

"Do you really think I want to be here? Do you really think I want to live in your old house? Boy, you've got it all wrong! I'd like to be as far away from here as possible. I'm only here because my dad says I have to, not because I want to." The jerk made me mad. Here I was trying to be nice to him, and he was telling me to get out of his face. "Get your dumb boxes out of my room, like your mother said!"

He started to say something but stopped when he heard Pamela coming down the hall. He sneered at me, and picked up the nearest box. My anger disappeared then as fast as it had come, and I felt sad and lonely again. I don't want to fight with Joey. I want us to be friends. Somehow I have to stop getting so angry at him.

The Journey

The Oskeet River:

The clouds had rolled in fast: dark, fierce clouds that covered any trace of blue sky. Watching the swirling grayness, Kate thought of her dad and how he had always told her to head for camp when a storm threatened. He would expect them back by now and be worrying.

Kate knew her dad would start searching for them, but searching up the north branch of the Oskeet. It was the way they had always gone before. He would canoe miles the wrong way before turning around. Kate hoped he would be okay. With the coming storm, it wasn't safe even for an expert canoer like her dad to be out on the water.

It wasn't raining yet, but she could see that the sky undoubtedly had some serious rain in mind. After the bright sunshine of a couple of hours before, the dark clouds scared her. And the wind wasn't making her feel any better. The earlier summer breeze was now a minigale, bending trees and bushes, whipping the water so that it bucked back and forth as if trying to rise out of the riverbed.

Kate shivered in her halter top and shorts, her shoul-

6 7

ders and neck twitching as the wind hit her. The temperature was dropping fast.

The stretcher poles were digging into her hands, blistering her fingers. She tried not to think about them and looked back over her shoulder at Joey. He was plodding along, cold and tired like her. They would have to stop soon for a rest.

Craning her head around a little farther, she saw the stick still clenched tightly between Linda's teeth. With the stretcher lurching from side to side, the broken leg was being constantly shaken, causing Linda a lot of pain. As loud as the wind was, there were times when Kate could here Linda moaning.

Kate told herself that when they turned the small bend up ahead, they would stop. She wanted to look at the splint. Maybe if she tightened the straps, Linda's leg wouldn't hurt her as badly.

They also had to stop for a drink. They hadn't had water since before they capsized. Kate's own throat was parched. They didn't need dehydration on top of everything else.

Kate didn't know if the river water was safe to drink. But since there were no factories or chemical plants upstream to dump junk into it, she thought it would be okay. They would have to risk it anyway. With their canteens lost in the rapids, river water was all they had.

When they finally rounded the bend, pushing through a small thicket of scrub pines, Kate felt what was left of her spirits shrivel away inside her. They stopped and stared in disbelief.

A big chunk of the riverbank directly in front of them was gone, eaten away possibly a thousand years before by the mouth of a creek. Twenty-five feet across with sides as steep as a playground sliding board, the creek looked impossible to cross.

Though Kate remembered canoeing past the creek on the way down, it hadn't seemed nearly as big to her then.

"Oh, Jeez!" she said. "We better put Linda down."

They lowered the stretcher to the ground and let go of the poles. She had been carrying Linda for more than an hour, and now the sudden lightness in Kate's arms felt strange.

"Linda looks sick, Kate." Joey was bent over the stretcher.

Kate knelt down beside her. Linda looked even paler than before. "How do you feel?" Kate asked.

Linda took the stick slowly from between her teeth and tried to smile. "Not so hot."

She was perspiring. Kate smoothed her hair and spoke as calmly as she could. "We stopped for just a couple of minutes. I'm going to get you some water to drink and check your splint, then we'll be going again."

Kate took the piece of cloth that she had used to cool Linda's forehead and walked toward the creek. She felt the muscle in her face twitching again. It only happened when she was worried. Like now, knowing it was her responsibility to get them back to camp, and not knowing if she could do it.

Kate knew what her dad would say, what he always said: "Do your best. You can't do more than that." He told her that before every swim meet. But this was more than a race. If they lost now, Linda might die.

Kate slid down the dirt and weeds of the bank to the edge of the water. Joey was still back with Linda. She called up to him to come and get a drink. As she cupped her hands under the water and brought them up to her mouth, she heard him sliding down the bank.

The water was cold and had a rooty taste. Kate drank several handfuls before stopping. Joey was still drinking, the water dribbling down his chin. He hadn't said much to her since calling her stupid. He hung his head now like an old doll she once had that had lost the stuffing out of its neck.

If Joey wasn't talking, Kate decided it was best that she not talk either. Maybe then they could avoid an argument. She rubbed the cloth back and forth in the creek, getting it as clean as she could, then let it soak up as much water as possible.

Climbing back up the bank, Kate had to dig the sides of her sneakers into the dirt. The riverbank was so steep, it was the only way she could get a footing.

As she knelt down beside Linda, Kate said, "I soaked this cloth in the creek. I'm going to give you a drink by letting the water drip into your mouth, okay?" Linda nodded her head slightly and opened her mouth. As the thin stream of water fell between her lips, Linda swallowed thirstily.

"There's a creek up ahead that we're going to have to cross. But there's no need to worry." The twitching she still felt in her cheek told Kate she was doing enough worrying for both of them. The cloth was now dry. "I'm going to soak this again, and give you another drink."

Down by the water, Joey was washing his face. Kate dipped the cloth into the river while looking at him. She had to say something. It was stupid not to talk to each other.

"Joey, why are you so quiet? Are you feeling okay?"

He flashed a look at her, then stood up to dry his face on the end of his shirt. In that instant, before he said anything, she saw the fear in his eyes.

"How are we going to get Linda across that creek? We'll drop her!"

Joey would deny it, but Kate could see how hard he was trying not to cry. He was scared. So why should I be surprised, she thought. I'm scared too.

Kate knew herself well enough to know she was going to be nice to Joey. Grudges just didn't last long with her, especially when the other kid felt bad. After all, she told herself, it won't do any good if he panics and does something stupid.

"Hey, we'll get Linda across. Don't worry about it! It'll be a bit of work, but we'll do it." Kate tried to sound positive, as if there was no possibility in the world anything could go wrong.

"Look, I'm going to check out the creek. Why don't you take this cloth up to Linda and drip the water into her mouth so she gets another drink?"

He took the cloth from her, looking at it and holding it like it was something fragile, being careful not to squeeze the water out.

"Kate, I'm tired." Joey turned toward her, his wet hair making a fringe around his unsmiling face. "I don't think I can carry Linda all the way back to camp." He had been doing his best not to let it happen, but now tears burst into his eyes. "I don't want her to die." Sobbing, his chest heaving up and down, he turned away.

Whenever one of her friends cried, Kate would put her arms around her and hug her, but with Joey she didn't. She was sure that if she tried, he would push her away. How could he let someone he hated hug him? So Kate just stood at the edge of the river and talked to him.

"We'll make it. I'm tired too, but we'll stop and rest as often as we have to. We'll get Linda back to camp. I know we will."

Joey wiped his eyes, then knelt down and dipped the cloth back into the river. When he stood up, he said with his head still turned away, "Sorry, I acted like a baby."

"It's a really hard time. But we'll make it. You okay?"

He climbed up the bank without answering.

Not knowing what to do about Joey, Kate went to look at the creek. Maybe just getting across will help him feel better, she told herself.

As she walked along the edge of the bank, Kate could see that it would be easier to cross if they followed the stream fifty feet back into the trees. They would still have to wade through water, but it wouldn't be as deep or as wide. She thought they could do it. Anyway, what choice do we have? We have to keep going, she told herself.

Joey was wiping Linda's face with the wet cloth when Kate got back. "She passed out. I'm really worried about her. Do you think she has a fever?"

Kate put her hand on Linda's forehead. "I don't know. Maybe a slight one. But I don't think it's bad. Let me check her splint, then we'd better go." She didn't like how pale Linda looked, or that she had passed out again. But Kate knew she couldn't tell Joey. He would get more upset if she did. Freaking out wasn't going to help anything.

The splint seemed tight enough on Linda's leg. Kate couldn't see any place where it was loose. As far as she could tell it was keeping the broken bones from moving around.

"It looks okay to me, Joey. I don't know what else we can do, except to get going."

They picked up the stretcher, the wood digging again into their hands. The muscles in Kate's shoulders and arms started their familiar aching.

They carried the stretcher along the bank to a spot where the drop to the creek wasn't as great.

"Let's put Linda down close to the edge. Okay, now climb down into the stream." The water was freezing, and their sneakers quickly soaked through.

"Carefully pick up your end of the stretcher the same time I pick up mine." They struggled with it, straining, but they managed to lift the stretcher with Linda up off the bank, handling it awkwardly until it was between them.

"Watch out for the stones along the creek bottom. They can be slippery." Joey nodded his head.

They walked sideways across the creek, the stretcher with Linda on it hanging between them. They were almost to the middle when Joey fell.

From Kate Evans's Diary:
FRIDAY, JUNE 15

*A*ll this afternoon, I worked hard unpacking and arranging my stuff. The room won't look good until the walls are painted and new curtains hung. But at least it isn't so gloomy. With my bed and bureau and desk and posters of my favorite rock groups, I feel now like I'm surrounded by old friends.

Today was really hot, ninety-two degrees, the radio said. And the little fan Mrs. Morgan, I mean Pamela, propped in the open window wasn't doing much. About four o'clock, I'd had it and decided to get a shower. I padded down the hall in my bare feet to the bathroom and closed the door behind me. I was finally alone, away from everyone asking me how my room was coming along, away from Joey sticking his head in and belching. I'd tried to be friendly and laughed each time he did it, but it wasn't funny. Now, I could stop being phony and just relax.

I turned on the shower and started to undress. Getting out of my sweaty clothes felt really good. I was unhooking my bra when—bang—the bathroom door swings open and slams against the wall. The suddenness startled me. It was Joey.

"Wow! Look at you! Sexy!" he said and leaned against the door, wolf-whistling.

"Get out of here!" I yelled, pulling a towel up in front of me.

"I need a drink of water. I'm thirsty," was Joey's excuse, and he grabbed a glass off the sink.

"Get out of here! Get out of here!" I kept yelling. I was furious and began pushing him.

"Hey, let me get a drink!" The water was splashing all around as he tried to get the glass to his mouth.

"Get out of here! Get your drink downstairs!" I yelled.

He just stood there pressed against the sink, laughing. Then he started pulling at my towel and wolf-whistling again.

I was fighting to keep the towel around me when Pamela and Linda hurried into the bathroom.

"What's going on?" Pamela shouted. "Joey, let go of Kate's towel!" She pulled him by the arm out into the hallway. "Now, what happened? No, let Kate tell me!"

I took a deep breath to try to calm down, then explained what had happened.

"Joey, is that right?" Pamela looked at him.

"All I wanted was a drink of water, Mom."

"Joey, how could you be so rude? Go to your room until dinnertime!" She watched him slouch off down the hall, then came back into the bathroom and put an arm around me.

"I'm sorry, Kate. I guess Joey just isn't used to having another sister. With more people using the bathroom, we'll have to develop some rules. But for now, dear, you go and take your shower. Dinner will be ready in about an hour." She smiled and kissed me on the cheek.

After she left, Linda stayed and helped wipe up the water Joey'd spilled.

"Joey gets kind of wild sometimes." She turned toward me. "But he really is an okay kid." She was protecting her brother. Well, it was what I expected. She might like me, but in the pinch her brother came first.

"Yeah sure," I said.

"I'll see you downstairs."

After she'd gone, I closed the door and sat on the toilet seat. I folded my arms around me, pressing the towel against my chest, and let the tears come. My life has changed so quickly. I feel so alone. Will I ever be happy again?

The Oskeet River:

3:26 P.M., THURSDAY, JULY 12

*J*oey fell backward, the stretcher jerking and dipping, almost tipping over. But somehow Joey managed to hold on to it, keeping his end out of the creek. He was sitting in the water, the stretcher poles pressing into his shoulders. Kate strained to keep her end steady.

"Are you okay?"

"Yeah." He choked the word out. He was scared. Sweat was beading up on his face.

"Try to get up. But do it slowly."

"Okay."

He got up onto his knees, the water splashing about his chest. He grimaced as he forced his legs to push himself up, the weight of Linda and the stretcher pressing down on him.

Finally on his feet, he stood for a moment, breathing hard. They were both shaking. They had almost dropped Linda. And they still had another ten feet of creek to cross.

"Let's walk very slowly," Kate almost whispered to him.

Every small side step they took they ground their feet down into the loose stones and sand to get a secure footing. The trees and bushes were dense along the banks of the stream, cutting off the breeze from the river. The air was warmer and felt good to Kate, even with her feet slogging through the cold water.

When they finally reached the far side, they had to lift the stretcher to almost shoulder height before they could put Linda up on the bank. When they were sure she wouldn't roll off, they scrambled up the sand and dirt, holding on to roots to pull themselves up. Joey was completely soaked, and Kate's sneakers were belching water out their side holes.

Joey flopped onto the ground, breathing rapidly, and being very quiet. Kate put her head in her hands and closed her eyes. They had made it across. She couldn't believe how close they had been to dropping Linda. They needed to rest, but how could they? Now that they had made it to the other side of the creek, they had to keep going. Linda was depending on them.

"We better go," Kate said.

"No! I can't! I'll drop her!" A look of panic filled Joey's face. His eyes were stretched open so wide that his eyeballs looked like they would pop out. He was shaking, his body trembling all over.

"Joey, everything will be okay! We'll make it! We'll get Linda back." Kate was surprised at how worked up he was. She hadn't realized he was this upset.

"No! None of us will get back! We'll die here on this stinking river! Linda is too heavy. I can't carry her. I'm not strong enough."

"We're not going to die! Not Linda, not any of us!"

Kate wasn't really sure about Linda. She had been thinking about how people can go into shock and die. And every time Linda passed out, Kate was afraid that was what was happening. But there was no way she was going to tell that to Joey.

"We'll stop and rest as many times as we need to. But we will get Linda back to camp. We will!"

"Look at us!" Joey was standing now, his face flushed, moving restlessly from one foot to the other. "We're wet, there's a storm coming, and"—he waved his arm in the direction they were going—"and we've got miles and miles of these trees and bushes, and we don't know how many more creeks we have to slop through."

As he talked, Kate got up from where she had been sitting and moved toward him. Maybe if I put my arms around him I can calm him down, she told herself. Her dad used to do that with her when she got upset. But Joey kept backing away, and when she finally reached out to take his arm and hold him still, he swung at her.

"Get away from me! If you hadn't taken us down this stupid river, we wouldn't be in this mess! It was your stupid idea!" he yelled. "If Linda dies, it will be your fault!"

He was gulping air fast, as if he were hyperventilating. Kate remembered a kid in school hyperventilating, and then having to breathe into a paper bag because he got too much oxygen. If Joey hyperventilated, she didn't have a bag for him.

"And if she dies, I'll kill you!"

He's really letting it loose, Kate thought. And maybe she could understand it, but she sure wasn't ready for it. Not here, not now.

"Joey, you've got to stop this." Kate reached out to try to touch him again. Too late she realized it was the wrong thing to say and wrong thing to do. He exploded, charging at her and knocking her to the ground.

"I hate you! I hate you!"

He was on top of her, punching her and screaming. Kate tried to cover her face as best she could while pushing to get him off. She didn't want to hurt him, but when his fist hit her nose and blood trickled out, that did it.

Kate punched him in the stomach and heaved herself up, forcing him off her onto the ground. He lay there holding his stomach and crying, big sobs coming from his chest.

Kate's nose hurt and she was mad, so she left him lying on the ground and went back down to the creek. She washed the blood off her face, and put her head back to stop any more bleeding. Jeez, what am I going to do? she asked herself. Somehow, Joey has to stop this stuff. They would never get Linda back if he kept freaking out. The brat only thought about himself.

Her nose was still throbbing when she climbed up the bank. If she had to, Kate was ready to sit on Joey and shake some sense into his fat head.

He was gone. Linda was still lying on the stretcher, but Joey was gone.

From Kate Evans's Diary:

S U N D A Y ,   J U N E   2 4

*T*his morning, Linda and I painted my bedroom a bright raspberry. The color was pretty and seemed to make the room really mine. I felt better about things. Joey and I'd been staying out of each other's way. And as long as he and I weren't getting into it, Linda wasn't being defensive with me. I started to think that maybe living in the house might just work. It didn't take long to find out how wrong I was.

When Linda went to make a phone call, I flopped down on my old familiar bed. Maybe the bedrooms keep changing, but at least my bed stays the same, like a good friend. Snuggling into my pillow and comforter made me feel warm and secure.

I was tired. We'd worked hard, starting right after breakfast and not stopping until just before noon. I could feel a gentle breeze blowing across me from the open window. My eyes closed and I burrowed my head down into my pillow.

I was drifting off to sleep, the world all sweet and dreamy. And then, sound, tremendous sound. Like an explosion inside my head. A fire siren? A bomb? I fought my way out of sleep. Somehow, I had to stop the screeching. I jerked awake, banging my head against the wall.

"Get up! Get up! Time to get up! No sleeping on the job!" It was Joey. He was standing in my doorway laughing.

"Boy, you should have seen you jump. You must have jumped three feet," he said. He was holding a trumpet in his hand.

"You creep! Get that horn out of my room!"

"I'm not in your room. I'm in the hall. What's wrong? Don't you like music?"

"Music I like, noise I don't. I was trying to sleep."

"Sleep? Sleep? What are you, lazy or something? No one lazy is allowed in this house. Don't you know that?" He laughed a nerdy laugh, then blowing his trumpet walked backward down the hall to his room.

He was playing something that sounded like "Old MacDonald Had a Farm" but with a lot of car horns mixed in. He was blowing the trumpet so loud I was getting a headache. And outside, I could hear Bear howling, letting the world know what he thought about Joey's trumpet playing.

I lay on my bed thinking. Why is he so inconsiderate of people and dogs? Doesn't he care? Maybe it's just me he doesn't care about. That makes sense. Yeah, he's been staying out of my way, but he still makes it pretty obvious that he'd be happier if he'd never met me. Well, he isn't going to chase me away with his tin trumpet. If he can have "fun" with me, I can have fun with him.

I waited until I heard him stop practicing, if that's what you'd call it, and go into the bathroom. Then quietly, I got off my bed and walked quickly down the hall to his room. It was such a mess. He had stuff all over the place. I almost tripped over a baseball bat, then a set of weights, then an empty glass, all spread across the floor like land mines. I missed stepping on each of them by sheer luck.

The trumpet lay on his bed. I picked it up. I had to be fast. He'd be coming back any second. Looking around for something I could use, I saw a sock sticking out from under his bureau. I grabbed it and rammed it down as far as I could inside the trumpet. If he didn't look into the end of the horn, he wouldn't see it.

The toilet was flushing as I tiptoed down the hall. I just got inside my door when Joey came out of the bathroom. I covered my mouth with my hand. I didn't want him to hear me laughing.

Would he pick up his trumpet again and try to blow it? He did. I could hear him, the funny noise of air escaping from his mouth like he was trying to blow up a balloon with a hole in it. I couldn't keep it in. I let out a burst of laughter. He heard me cause he yelled and came thumping his feet down the hall. I hid my face behind a book.

"Kate, you stuck this sock in my trumpet didn't you!" He came into my room waving his sock.

I looked at him as innocently as I could. "I thought that last note was quite nice."

"You think you're so funny! You just wait!"

Before I could say anything, Pamela called up the stairs for us to come down for lunch. Perfect timing. I pushed myself up off the bed and brushed passed him. "Lunchtime, Joey."

"Yeah, yeah, I know. But don't you forget, I'll get you back!"

The Oskeet River:

*J*oey! Joey! Come back here!" Kate yelled into the trees in the direction she thought he must have gone. With the wind blowing as hard as it was, she didn't know if he heard her. But even if he could, chances were he wouldn't answer.

She stood on the riverbank, looking north, wishing she could see the camp, but seeing instead the gray-black water angrily chopping at the rocks. For the first time that she could remember, the river felt like a lonely and depressing place.

In her mind, Kate pictured Joey getting lost in the woods and not being found until a hunter tripped over his frozen body next winter. She kicked at a stone, sending it skipping across the ground into a bush.

"Great!" She shouted at the river. "I'll get back to camp, that is if I do get back, with one stepsister in a coma, and one stepbrother missing and presumed dead. Everybody will love that. And everybody will say it's my fault, just like Joey said." Her voice had dropped to a whisper. There were tears on her cheeks.

Kate wiped her hands down her face, feeling suddenly very tired. She couldn't leave Linda to look for

Joey. There was nothing else to do but try to carry Linda by herself. She walked back to where Linda lay on the stretcher. Maybe she's just asleep. That's possible.

"Don't assume the worst!" she told herself out loud. "Keep your head on! You'll drag Linda on the stretcher. And as long as she doesn't fall off, and as long as there are no more creeks to cross, or dead trees to climb over, you'll make it." Talking to herself made her feel better.

Kate picked up her end of the stretcher, careful not to hold it so high that Linda would slide off, and started walking, dragging the other end of the stretcher through the dirt. It was hard going, a lot harder than she had first thought. She had to watch the ground closely, looking for the smoothest spots. But there were still stones and sticks hidden in the grass, and roots that jarred the stretcher and Linda's leg. But there was nothing else she could do.

Kate struggled to pull the stretcher, feeling more and more tired. She had to stop now every ten feet to rest before going on. Her breathing was so hard, she had to keep her mouth open to get enough air. And her shoulders and legs ached badly. She told herself that she would stop at the large pine tree just a few feet ahead, the one leaning out toward the river, then stop and take a longer rest.

"You want me to help?"

The voice came from the deep shadows of the pine tree. It came so unexpectedly, startling her, that Kate almost dropped the stretcher. She shut her eyes and took a deep breath to slow her heart's mad beating. She knew it was Joey. When she opened her eyes she saw him sitting on the ground, leaning against the tree.

"You jerk!" Kate yelled at him, all the anger and the fear she had been squashing down inside her bursting out. "You jerk! Leaving me and Linda was stupid! Don't you care what happens to her?"

Kate put the stretcher down, almost dropping it she was so angry, and limped on her aching legs to where he sat. Joey had no expression on his face. Reaching down, she grabbed him by his shirt and yanked him, trying to stand him on his feet, but he slipped and fell over.

"You stupid jerk!" Kate yelled, kicking him. "You want your sister dead like your father's dead? Is that what you want?"

That got a reaction. "Don't you talk about my father!" Joey yelled back, pushing himself up to his feet. "Don't you ever talk to me about my father! Do you hear me!" He was shaking his fist at her.

"Your father's dead. There's nothing you can do—"

Before Kate could finish, Joey roared as though his arm was being torn off and charged at her, swinging his fists. He hit her once before she tripped him and jumped on his back, pinning him to the ground.

Joey went wild, trying to throw her off, screaming, cursing her, but Kate stayed on top of him. Eventually, he stopped thrashing about and lay on the ground breathing hard, his face in the dirt.

"Get off me," he muttered through clenched teeth.

"I get the message, Joey. You don't want me to talk about your dad cause his dying really upsets you."

"Shut up!" He bucked under her again.

"I understand a little bit. Maybe my mom didn't die, but when she left my dad and me, and moved away, it was almost like she died."

"But she's not dead is she? You can still see her if you want to. You can still talk to her."

"She calls me at Christmas and on my birthday, and we talk for maybe five minutes. Yeah, I can still talk to her, if you call that talking. But I haven't seen her in more than two years, and sometimes I forget what she looks like. I have to look at her picture to remember." Kate stopped. She could feel her throat getting tight. She still got upset talking about her mother. Joey lay quietly on the ground beneath her, as if he might be listening.

"I've got a picture of my dad," Joey said. "Mom took it just before he went up in the plane. I didn't want him to go." He stopped with a choking sound.

"Why didn't you want him to go?"

Kate heard him swallowing as if he was having trouble talking.

"I had this dream, a stupid dream, that the plane was going to crash. He didn't believe me when I told him. He just laughed."

Joey was crying now with deep, chest-wrenching sobs. Kate moved off him and sat on the ground. She kept her hand on his back and rubbed him across the shoulders, hoping maybe she was comforting him.

"Do you think it was your fault?" Kate asked as gently as she could.

Joey pushed himself up onto his knees, trying to get his breath between the deep sobs that still came. He shook his head.

"No . . ." He fought to get his breath. "I'm just mad . . . I'm mad that he didn't believe . . . me." Tears rolled down his face. "And I miss him."

He started crying harder than ever. This time, without thinking about it, Kate put her arms around him and held him. And he let her, laying his head on her shoulder. And she cried too, missing her mother who was as lost to her as Joey's dad was to him.

They stayed like that for what seemed a long time. They stayed like that until there were no more tears and no more sobs, until they both felt better, calmer. Then, without saying anything, they both got up and walked over to Linda.

They picked up the stretcher and began again to

weave their way through the bushes and trees along the riverbank. Kate listened to the wind as it blew through the tops of the pine trees. It made a plaintive moaning sound that somehow reminded her of the awful noise Joey made with his trumpet.

From Kate Evans's Diary:

SUNDAY, JUNE 24

Today at lunch, I had to sit across the table from Joey again. It's quickly becoming my regular seat. I hate looking up from my plate and seeing his face smirking at me. I just try to ignore him the best I can. As usual, Dad and Pamela were sitting next to each other at the other end of the table. We had just started eating our tuna fish sandwiches, Joey giving me dirty looks about what I did to his trumpet, when Dad clanged the side of his glass with a spoon. Dad is so dramatic.

"Okay, guys. Pamela and I have a surprise for you. We're all going camping! What do you think of that?" He was beaming. One thing about Dad, he likes to camp more than just about anything. And Pamela must have caught his enthusiasm cause her eyes actually shone with excitement.

"Camping? Ugh, who wants to go camping?" Joey said, making one of his faces. "That's for Boy Scouts."

"Joey! Camping will be fun! Tom and Kate have done a lot of camping. They'll show us what to do."

I knew Pamela would have to do better than that if she wanted to sell Joey on camping. And not so deep down, I hoped she wouldn't succeed. I love to camp, but camping with Joey isn't my idea of fun.

"Sure, and what about the lions and bears? Are we going to bring them lunch, or are we going to be their lunch?" He had a smirk on his face.

"Joe, you're right." Dad is the only one who calls him Joe. "There are a few cougars in the mountains. But, sad to say, they're becoming extinct, so there aren't many left. And there are also some brown bears and even timber wolves. And yes, they can be dangerous. But they don't usually come down along the Oskeet River where we'll be camping, not unless something like a forest fire drives them down. So don't worry, we'll be okay.

"And you know what, we're going to have a great time. We'll take our canoe and explore the river. Kate is a good canoeist. She'll show you how to do it," Dad said, smiling happily.

Joey let out a moan. "Oh, great! Just what I need, a girl with wire teeth teaching me how to canoe."

It was the first time he'd said anything about the braces on my teeth. I should have known he'd say something about them sooner or later.

"Joey, apologize to Kate! That was very unkind!" Pamela said, getting up from her chair.

"Mom, I'm only thinking about my safety. Just think, what would happen if there was a thunderstorm? Lightning would strike her aluminum-plated choppers and she'd reach over and grab me. And there I'd be, cooked meat. You wouldn't want that for your son would you?" He laughed, jerking his body back and forth like he was being electrocuted.

I felt so hurt and angry, I just wanted to be away from him. I jumped up from the table, my hand swinging out and knocking my glass of milk over. The milk poured across the table, soaking my sandwich and everything else.

"You're a real slob, Kate, a real slob," Joey said as nasty as he could.

I don't know why I did it except I wanted to hit him. I picked up my glass with the little bit of milk that remained in it, and threw the milk at him. White drops speckled his face and shirt.

"You jerk!" Joey yelled.

"Kate! Joey! Stop it!" Dad and Pamela were now both on their feet. They pulled us away from the table. Dad had me by the arm, and Pamela had Joey.

"You two stop this fighting! Do you hear me?" Dad wasn't yelling, but his voice was sure loud and angry.

Linda was still sitting in her chair, frowning while she mopped up my spill with napkins. There she was in the middle again, feeling protective of Joey, yet wanting, I was sure, for everybody to get along. I felt bad. Why do I let him upset me? I wish he didn't make me so angry.

"Kate, I want you to tell Joe you're sorry you threw milk into his face."

I felt like a little kid being made to apologize. But

I'd acted like a little kid, so I guess I deserved to be treated like one. I looked at Joey, at the frown on his face.

"Joey, I'm sorry I threw the milk at you. I shouldn't have done it."

"Now, Joey, you apologize to Kate for the things you said!" Though angry, Pamela's eyes were filling with tears as if she was about ready to cry. I could see how important it is to her that we get along. She really wants us to be a family.

"No! I won't apologize to her! I hate her!" Joey yelled the words so loud he startled me. "I wish she'd never come here! I wish she'd go away!" He jerked his arm loose from Pamela and ran into the kitchen. A second later the screen door slammed.

Everyone stood still, not saying anything; then Pamela really did begin to cry. Dad went and put his arms around her, and she buried her face against his chest. She was crying so hard that she was almost choking when I heard her say, "It's not working out. What are we going to do?"

I feel terrible.

The Oskeet River:

7:10 P.M., THURSDAY, JULY 12

The last time they had stopped was about an hour before, but it felt to Kate like they had been walking forever. Her legs and arms ached so much she had permanent tears in the corners of her eyes.

The sun had gone down behind the trees some time ago. And in the quickly fading light, the overcast sky was growing very dark, making it hard to see. Kate knew they would have to stop soon. They just couldn't keep going. Under an overcast sky, there would be no stars or moon. The night would be pitch black. If they forced themselves to keep walking, she knew they would end up falling over a root or something and hurting Linda, maybe even falling into the river.

"Joey, I see a small clearing up ahead. We'll stop there. It'll be night soon," Kate said, calling back to him over her shoulder.

"Okay," he answered. She could tell by his voice that he was tired too. They needed to rest.

The clearing was small, no more than ten feet across, but it had overhanging trees that would give them some shelter from the wind and the rain when it came. They carried Linda to the back of the clearing and lowered her to the ground. She looked worse. Her skin was even paler than before. Kate picked up the piece of cloth from where it lay beside her, and went to the edge of the river to wet it.

Turning to climb back up the bank, Kate was surprised to see raspberries growing in a protected hollow. They were the first berries she'd seen that she knew they could eat. She picked a handful of the ripest ones, and carried them to Linda.

"I found raspberries growing down by the river. They'll give you some sugar. Please try to eat some." Linda had been conscious now for a while. And even if she was too weak to speak, having her awake made Kate feel better.

Linda opened her mouth partway, and Kate fed her the berries one at a time, letting each dissolve before giving her the next. When they were all gone, Kate dripped the water from the cloth in between Linda's lips. She gave her drinks twice more before Linda turned her face to the side. Kate wanted desperately to keep going to get Linda to a doctor, but it was getting too dark to see. She knew it wouldn't be safe.

She moved closer to Joey. "Are you okay?" she asked. He was sprawled on his back, his eyes staring straight up into the trees.

"I didn't think I could ever be so hungry. What I'd do for a cheeseburger, fries, and a Pepsi, you don't know. I keep looking for a McDonald's every time we go around a bend in the river."

Kate laughed. Joking was a good sign he was handling things better. "Yeah, my stomach's been grumbling for hours. Wait, I'll be back in a minute."

When Kate returned, she had both hands full of raspberries.

"Hamburgers and fries sure sound a lot better, but I'm afraid these will have to do."

"Next to a cheeseburger or maybe a pepperoni pizza, raspberries are my favorite food! Let me at them!" Joey smacked his lips.

It seemed funny to Kate, the two of them sitting in the growing dark, eating raspberries, talking instead of yelling. It was like being with any other kid. She looked at him, barely seeing his gray shape against the tree.

"How come you hate me?" she asked.

He was quiet for a minute; then shrugging his shoulders, he said, "I don't know. Maybe I don't hate you. Like I said before, maybe I'm just mad about what happened to my dad. Anyway, that's what the shrink says."

"You saw a shrink!" She had never known anyone who had seen a psychiatrist before.

"Yeah." He hung his head. "Mom made me go." He hesitated. "Anyway, the shrink said I'm mad at my dad, mad at him for not believing me about my dream and going and dying in the plane, instead of staying with us. The shrink said because my dad is dead, I have to be angry at somebody else. So maybe that's why I've been angry at you."

This is heavy stuff, Kate thought to herself. "Do you really think that's what's been happening?" she asked.

He didn't answer right away, but then, still looking at the ground, he mumbled, "Maybe, I don't know."

Kate couldn't see him crying, but she could hear sniffling noises.

"My dad was stupid. Why didn't he listen to me, Kate? Why?"

Joey wanted her to give him an answer, but she didn't know what to say. So she felt her way across the clearing to him and found his hand and held it.

"Kate, he didn't believe me!"

"He believed you loved him, Joey. He just didn't believe your dream could predict the future." Kate hesitated. She hoped she was telling him the right stuff. "Your dad most likely thought your dream meant you loved him and you'd miss him, nothing else."

"He was stupid!" Joey wailed out into the dark clearing.

"No, he wasn't. Most people don't think more than two seconds about dreams. Look, if I had a dream about you getting run over by a bus, would you believe me? Well, would you?"

"I guess not."

"See. How do we know what a dream means, if it means anything at all? They're strange, weird, spooky things." Kate thought of her own dream about her mother. "I'm always glad to forget them, if I can. Your dad loved you, and it's okay to miss him, but why be angry at him? He didn't mean to die."

For a long time, Joey cried, and Kate held him against her. With her arm around him, she thought about her mother, and wondered if her mother ever thought about her, if her mother sometimes missed her.

Night was almost completely upon them. Kate could barely see Joey now, even though he was right next to her. He was shivering. She was cold herself, her teeth chattering. The temperature felt like it had dropped another ten degrees. The afternoon had been chilly, especially when the wind caught them, but now it was downright cold. And they didn't have any shelter from it.

"Joey, let's move closer to Linda. Maybe if we huddle together we can all stay warmer. And if we pile pine needles alongside Linda, we can lie on them instead of the ground."

It wasn't very comfortable lying pressed against the stretcher, but Kate felt a bit warmer, and the pine needles gave a little cushion. She laid her head down on her bent arm, and gradually felt herself begin to relax. The stretcher pole was digging into her chest, but she was hardly aware of it, she was so tired.

Kate's right arm was across Linda's chest. Joey's arm, coming from the other side, was against hers. Linda was asleep, her chest rising and falling with shallow breaths. Kate felt better knowing Linda was comfortable enough to sleep. She listened to Joey breathing through his mouth. It was a peaceful, lulling sound.

Kate knew she couldn't have been asleep for long when she jerked awake. Someone was tugging her arm. For a moment, she didn't know where she was. Everything was pitch black. She was frightened and pulled her arm free.

"Kate! Kate!" It was Joey calling to her, shaking her. "Something's wrong with Linda! She's moaning!"

Kate shook the sleep out of her head and pushed herself up onto her knees. Reaching out, she felt for Linda. She was thrashing from side to side, moaning from what must have been terrible pain. The night was so black Kate couldn't see a thing. She had to feel her way to Linda's forehead. Linda was burning up with fever.

"Joey, she has a fever!" Kate talked in a rush, her stomach tightening into a knot. "I'm going to wet the cloth and wash her down, then we've got to go! We'll have to find our way in the dark, but we've got to get her back! Linda needs a doctor really badly."

Kate found the cloth beside Linda on the stretcher and crawled down the bank to the river. The night air was much colder by the water. As she soaked the cloth, she looked up toward the sky. There was absolutely no light, no stars, no moon. It was like she was blind.

How were they ever going to be able to carry Linda along the riverbank in the pitch blackness?

Kate felt her way back to Linda and washed her face, neck, and arms. She was so hot. Kate didn't know what else to do except wash her down.

"Joey, we'll have to keep washing her down. Here's the cloth. Will you soak it again for me?" He took the cloth and scurried off. He moved so fast Kate knew he was scared. She tested the vines that tied the life jackets to the stretcher poles. They seemed to be holding.

She heard Joey fall coming back up the bank. He mumbled something she couldn't make out, then came crawling through the river scrubs. She called his name to let him know where she was in the darkness.

"Here's the cloth, Kate." She took it from him and began washing Linda down again. "Is she going to die?" His voice sounded hoarse.

He hadn't asked her that since they first found Linda by the rapids. Until now, as bad as it was, they seemed to be making progress. But with Linda worse, and the woods and river absolutely black around them, everything looked hopeless. Kate put her hand on his arm.

"We're doing all we can for her, Joey. I don't know how bad she is. I only know we have to get her to a doctor. It's going to be hard. We'll have to feel our way along the bank, going very slowly to make sure we don't fall and drop Linda." He didn't say anything.

Impulsively, Kate put her arms around him and

hugged him. He hugged her back. They held onto each other tightly. All they had right then was each other. After a few seconds, they dropped their arms and felt their way to the stretcher. Kate didn't know if the hug helped Joey, but she knew she felt a little better. Some of the bad feelings that had been there between them seemed to have gone.

With Linda suspended between them on the stretcher, they walked very slowly out of the clearing toward the water. When Kate felt the bank slope sharply, she turned upriver, feeling each step she took by sliding her foot along the ground. It was going to take a long time to go even a short distance. She stumbled over a root but caught herself in time.

Kate felt like she was walking through a lightless tunnel, unable to see either the beginning or the end. Her eyes were useless. She had to rely on the touch of her feet and her hearing. She listened to the river flowing past on her right. Its gurgling noises, as it rushed over rocks, helped her to keep her bearings.

Every little while they came up against a tree that had fallen across the bank. If it was narrow, they would step over it very carefully. But if it was wide or had a lot of branches, Kate had to lead them around it. The worst part was the branches that whipped at her face and chest, leaving welts and cuts. After the first time a branch whipped her cheek, Kate kept her head bent to protect her eyes.

She was cold and tired. The little rest and the few berries she had had were not enough. Her strength was draining away. It felt to her as if they must have been walking, sliding their feet along the ground, for a couple of hours. Every now and again Kate heard and felt Joey stumble, but he never fell.

How long can we keep going? Kate asked herself. They had to stop, if just for five minutes, to rest. If they didn't rest for just a bit, they would be too tired to carry Linda, and, at some point, they would fall for sure. Kate knew Linda was terribly hurt, but they wouldn't make it, they wouldn't get her back, unless they rested for five or ten minutes. She stopped and looked over her shoulder toward Joey, knowing he was there though she couldn't see him.

"We better stop for a couple of minutes, or we're going to drop."

"Yeah, my arms feel like they're dead."

"Let's put Linda down."

Kate sat on the ground beside the stretcher and put her hand on Linda's forehead. She was still hot. Kate forced herself to crawl down the bank to the river and soak the piece of cloth in the water. After she had washed Linda's face and arms, she lay back on some pine needles to rest for just a couple of minutes. She lay there in the night's blackness, the sounds of the river and the wind growing faint in her mind.

From Kate Evans's Diary:
TUESDAY, JULY 3

*T*his afternoon, Linda and I played tennis on the courts by the high school. Being used to winning in my swim meets, this was a lesson in humility.

Linda served the ball across the net. I charged, swinging my racket, and drove the ball as usual too hard. It hit the court just outside the baseline. Another game, another set, another match lost. As I walked over to my towel to wipe the sweat off my face, Linda came jogging up.

"I wish I had your forehand. You have so much power! And you're so quick!" She smiled at me as she pushed strands of her long, blond hair back behind her ears. Linda always has something kind to say.

"But I always hit the ball too hard, and I just can't control where it goes like you can. You're such a good tennis player. I'm sorry I didn't give you much of a match."

"Oh, I really like playing with you. It's a lot of fun. Anyway, I've been playing longer than you have. Let's go home and get showers. I feel so hot!"

"And a Coke. I want to drink something cold!" I put my racket in its case. "I have so much fun with you, Linda. It's like I've known you my whole life, like we're real sisters."

She reached over and squeezed my hand. "We do have fun together, don't we? Like you, I wasn't sure at first, but now I'm glad you and your dad are living with us."

We began walking back toward the house. "I wish I could get along with Joey half as well. I try to laugh at his jokes and kid with him. And I've even tried staying out of his way. But he still doesn't like me."

Linda was staring at the ground as we walked. "I don't know why Joey's so nasty to you. He never used to be like that." She stopped and looked at me.

"No, that's not true. He took Dad's death very hard. I remember he kept asking why Dad didn't listen to him about some stupid dream. He was miserable. Then one day, I found him in the garage, sitting on the little red wagon Dad used to pull him around in when he was small. He was crying. I don't think he'd ever cried for Dad until then. After that, he didn't seem to be so angry. At least until . . ." She paused and then went on. "Well, you know." She shrugged her shoulders. "I guess he wants his life to always be the same, and if it's not he can't accept it."

"Sounds like you're talking about me. I've a hard time accepting things changing too." I remembered how I yelled and cried and slammed doors when Dad told me I'd have to leave Warren High and my friends.

"But, Kate, you did accept the changes. Joey hasn't. Maybe he still hasn't gotten over our dad's death, maybe that's the problem. Do you know he still talks about that dream he had?"

We walked along together for a couple of minutes, not saying anything, just feeling the morning sun shining hot on our faces.

"Linda, I don't know if I've accepted anything," I finally said. "But since I moved in, you and your mother have been great, making me feel welcome. I feel unhappy only those times when Joey and I get into it. After something happens, like last week, I think that maybe I should just leave, go away somewhere. The house would be so much more peaceful without us fighting."

Linda grabbed my arm. "Don't ever think of that! It just takes time. Joey will change. He'll get to like you. And you'll get to like him. Give it time. Mom told me she'd read somewhere that it can take two or three years for a stepfamily to feel like it's a real family."

"Two or three years! Jeez, I don't know if we'll make it that long. I think we might end up strangling each other," I said, then laughed to hide how worried I really felt.

"I know you and Joey will work it out. I just know it."

Linda sounded so positive. Maybe she's right, I remember thinking. Maybe it's just a matter of time. Hang in there. Don't let it get me down, and just keep trying to get along with Joey. Anyway, what else can I do?

When we got back to the house, Linda went up first to get a shower. And after I drank a can of Coke in the kitchen, I jogged upstairs myself. We'd left all the windows and doors open to let the morning breezes blow through the house, including my own bedroom door. But now, it was closed. Blown shut by the wind I was sure.

As soon as I opened the door, my stomach tightened up so fast I could hardly breathe. Instantly, I felt like I was going to be sick. I couldn't focus on anything in the room. It was a horrible jumble. Trashed. My room had been trashed. My records and tapes thrown everywhere. The curtains yanked down and tangled on my bed. My newly painted walls, my rug, and my mirror scribbled on with black marker. Then I saw my pretty ceramic lamp, the one my grandmother gave me when I was nine, lying smashed in the corner.

I fell sobbing to my knees. Linda heard me and came running from the bathroom, a towel wrapped around her. I heard her gasp.

"Oh, Kate! This is awful! How could anyone do this?" She dropped down beside me and put her arm around me. "Let's find Mom. I think she's across the street at the Coopers. She needs to know." She pulled me to my feet. "Come to my room while I get dressed. Then we'll get Mom."

I started to walk down the hall with her, upset, my thoughts all mixed up. My room was so pretty, I said to myself. Why was it all ruined? It had to be Joey. He said he hated me and would get me back. I didn't know what to do. I felt hurt and angry. I wanted suddenly to be as far away as possible. I didn't care where I went. I just needed to get away. I pulled loose from Linda and ran back down the hall to the stairs.

"Kate, come back! Don't leave! We've got to find Mom!" I heard her calling after me, but I didn't want to hear. I couldn't believe anymore that everything was going to be all right.

I ran down the stairs and out the front door. I didn't think about where I was going. I just went. For the first time in my life, I was running away.

The Oskeet River:
5:43 A.M., FRIDAY, JULY 13

*S*light drizzle woke her, the cold drops landing softly on her face. Kate sat up with a start. It was morning. A gray light was seeping through the trees, revealing the water-laden clouds overhead and the dark shapes of the scrub pines along the riverbank.

They had fallen asleep. The realization made her jump to her feet. She turned around quickly looking for Joey, her heart thumping madly. He was asleep at the base of a tree, lying on his stomach, his face tucked into his bent arm.

"Joey! Wake up!" Kate shouted and ran to him. "Wake up! We fell asleep!" As she shook him, he turned over onto his back, his eyes opening and focusing on her.

He sat up. "What?" The awfulness of what she was saying finally hit him. He looked anxiously around for the stretcher. "Is Linda okay?"

"I don't know." Kate hurried back to where they had left her and felt her forehead. "She still has a fever! She's still in a bad way! We have to get going. We've lost a lot of time."

Rubbing sleep from his eyes, Joey came stumbling over to the stretcher. "Okay, let's go."

When they picked up the stretcher, Kate could feel how her muscles had tightened up during the night. But her guilt about falling asleep made her ignore the soreness and stiffness and walk as fast as she could.

"Do you think we're anywhere near camp?" Joey yelled from behind her; his voice sounded anxious, as if he was feeling bad about having slept.

"I don't know," Kate yelled back over her shoulder. "But I'd guess we're still a few miles away. If we push on, and nothing happens, we should get there sometime today."

"That's good enough for me. I just hope it's good enough for Linda."

The rain was now falling steadily. Once they were out from under the trees, walking through the tall grass and scrubs, it didn't take long for their clothes to become soaked through. Before they had started, Kate had turned Linda's head to the side and covered her face enough with the cloth to keep the rain from filling her mouth and nose, and maybe drowning her. The best thing about the rain was that it would help to cool her down, keeping her fever from getting too high.

The morning seemed like evening under the thick black clouds. There was no color in the trees, or along the riverbank, and especially not in the river. Everything looked dull, as if it had been covered with gray paint.

Kate thought how strange it was that except for a

few birds she hadn't seen any animals. Usually, she would see at least raccoons and squirrels, often deer. But she hadn't seen any for more than a day. It was as if they sensed a disaster in the air and were escaping before it happened.

Lightning flashed in the distance, followed seconds later by the low rumble of thunder. The storm was a bad one, and coming straight toward them. With the wind blowing stronger, and the rain now pelting down, Kate moved farther in from the river to be closer to a row of trees. This gave them some protection from the wind at least.

It was becoming almost impossible to see. It seemed as if a waterfall had suddenly been dumped on them. The rain was falling so hard the stretcher poles were becoming slippery, making them difficult to hold.

At a wide dip in the riverbank, the trees and underbrush grew together so thickly that Kate and Joey had to force their bodies through the tangle of branches. Carrying the stretcher as high as their aching arms would let them, they tried to keep the branches from whipping back at Linda. Kate could feel Linda moving on the stretcher as if the pain from her broken leg was getting worse. The stretcher was beginning to shake.

Without thinking, not even knowing if Linda was conscious, but scared that she might drop her, Kate yelled back over her shoulder, "Linda, lie still!"

As soon as Kate said it, she felt ashamed. How could I be so unfeeling? she thought to herself. She pushed on, leading them blindly through the last of the thicket, collecting what seemed like a hundred scratches on her arms and legs. She was crying.

As soon as she could risk it, Kate looked back at Linda. "I'm sorry I yelled. I was just scared I'd drop you," she shouted to be heard over the storm, again not knowing if Linda was awake to hear her.

"I know you're hurting. I'm really sorry." She kept walking and crying. Why did I have to yell at her when she's so badly hurt? She had never yelled at Linda before.

Kate was so upset she didn't notice it at first. But then she felt it harder in the small of her back, a rubbing. She realized it was Linda's foot, the foot of her good leg. Linda was trying to stroke her, the only way she could let Kate know everything was okay.

Kate wanted badly to put the stretcher down and hug Linda. She wanted to let Linda know how much she meant to her. But instead she started walking faster. The best thing she could do for Linda was just keep going.

Kate blinked her eyes to stop her tears, though that did little good under the steady stream of water that poured over her face.

It was the rain, she realized, that must have cooled Linda down and wakened her, the rain that was now being driven by the wind straight through their already drenched clothes. She shivered as the cold water rolled down her back. As bad as the weather was, they had to keep going for Linda's sake. Help would never find them in the storm; somehow they would have to find it.

"Joey, are you okay?" Kate yelled to be heard over the rain and wind.

Looking back over her shoulder, she saw the same fear in his face that she felt, a fear that made her forget the pain of the stretcher poles cutting into her hands.

She knew Joey was three years younger than her, but with his brown curly hair pasted by the rain against his head, he looked even younger, like a little kid. Kate was surprised at how protective she suddenly felt toward him.

"Yeah, I'm okay," he yelled back, and he tried to smile as if to prove it. But the result was more of a wince under the pelting rain that stung his cheeks already reddened from the cold.

Kate smiled at him as reassuringly as she could. She wanted to hug him, like she wanted to hug Linda, and tell him she was sorry for the trouble between them. From all that they had told each other, she had a better idea of why the trouble had happened. Now, she wondered if they would get another chance to be like a real sister and brother. She wished they each hadn't been so scared to let the other into the family.

Kate frowned, bowed her head into the rain, and pushed into another thicket. They lifted the stretcher again as high as they could to clear as many branches as possible. They were beginning to skirt the edge of a tangle of brambles when a powerful bolt of lightning snapped the air above their heads. They stopped, scared silly by the noise and the blinding flash of light.

In that instant, Kate was sure she saw a pair of timber wolves not fifty feet from them, racing away through the underbrush, away from the lightning and the noise. She wondered what wolves were doing so near the river. Is the storm so bad it scared them down out of the mountains? Or are they tracking us? She didn't know what petrified her more, the lightning or the wolves. But there wasn't time then to think about it.

A second crack snapped the air, not as loud as the first and different, the sound of wood splitting, breaking. As they looked up, the top of a massive pine tree came crashing down through the smaller trees like a diver belly flopping. It thundered down toward them so fast they didn't have time to think to move. The decapitated treetop hit the ground no more than ten feet away, flipping broken branches all around them. They jumped back, almost dumping Linda out of the stretcher.

Kate looked at Joey. He was very pale. They had been lucky for a change. Stopping when the lightning first hit had saved them. If they had kept walking, she knew, they would have been crushed by the tree.

Kate took a deep breath and shouted back to him. "We better keep going."

It took Kate several minutes to find a way around the tree. The tip lay in the water and extended back through the brush more than thirty feet. They had to make a path inland from the river through tangles of wet branches until they reached the tree's jagged end, scorched black by the lightning.

Acrid, gray smoke rose from the burned wood. Kate's stomach suddenly felt queasy at the thought of how close they had come to disaster. She stopped for a second until the nausea passed, then made her rubbery legs lead them back to the riverbank.

The rain wasn't letting up. Kate felt miserable, slogging through the mud and sand, her arms and legs splattered with dirt, her sneakers soaking wet. She wanted desperately for it all to be over, or at least to know that they were getting close to camp. She fought down the depressed feelings she was getting, knowing that she couldn't let herself get discouraged. She knew that Linda might die if she didn't get medical help soon. They couldn't afford to stop anymore. As long as their legs still worked, they had to keep going, following the river back to camp.

Kate thought about her dad and Pamela. They had to be frantic, searching the river. But what could they or the rangers do at night or in the storm?

"Hey, Kate!" Joey yelled from behind her. "I think I remember those rocks. Weren't they near our camp?"

Kate looked toward the river and saw the rocks he meant. They were oddly shaped. Together, they looked like a large deformed dog, ears sticking straight back, legs out to the side. She vaguely remembered them. But she wasn't sure if she had seen them near camp or not. She was afraid to hope.

"I think I remember them too," she shouted back to Joey.

They started walking faster. Kate forgot about the open blisters on the back of her heels, and the pouring rain suddenly didn't seem so bad. She held the stretcher poles tighter and bulled ahead. She knew she shouldn't, she knew she should expect the worse, but she couldn't help thinking about camp and dry clothes and food.

They were going up a slight rise in the riverbank when she felt the tug, a downward pull on the right side of the stretcher; then Joey yelled.

"Kate! Stop! The stretcher is breaking!" The stretcher lurched to the right and Kate fell. They all fell, sliding down toward the river.

From Kate Evans's Diary:
T U E S D A Y ,   J U L Y   3

*T*onight, I walked more than a mile before I realized where I was going. I was going to Warren, where Dad and I had lived in our apartment. I didn't know why I was going there. I just was. I wasn't crying any longer, but my insides kept churning over and over. I kept trying to figure out how my life could change from being so very good to being so awful in just two months.

I didn't know what to do. But I told myself I couldn't go back. I wouldn't go back. I kept heading toward Warren, like I was being drawn there, to the old apartment that had been my home for so long, where I'd been happy. Maybe it didn't make sense, but I felt I just had to go there. For some strange reason, it was very important that I see it again. I started walking faster.

It was almost dark by the time I reached the town, but the stores were still open on Jones Avenue. I went into a Rite Aid drugstore and bought a Milky Way candy bar, a bag of potato chips, and a can of Pepsi. I was starved. I hadn't thought to bring my wallet. All I had was the two dollars I'd stuffed into the pocket of my shorts when I went to play tennis with Linda.

I ate as I walked, looking at every store and every

house, remembering it all. I missed the town, and all of my friends. Jeez, it was a neat place to live. I walked passed the high school, locked up and empty for the summer. The windows were blank, reflecting back the streetlights. Warren Memorial High School, where I'd spent two years of my life, sat there beyond its front lawn, just waiting for September and the first bell when the kids would charge in through the doorways. But I wouldn't be one of those kids.

I choked on the candy bar, and my eyes filled up with tears. Coughing, I started running down the sidewalk, not bearing to look at the school anymore, not wanting to remember.

The apartment wasn't far away. I turned down Maple Avenue like I'd done so many times, knowing all the places where tree roots pushed up the cement sidewalk blocks. And there it was, 119-B. Without thinking, I ran toward the front door just like I used to do, across the grass, past the lilac bushes.

I stopped. There were lights on inside. Someone was living there. For a long moment, I just stared, seeing the open window, the curtain rustling in the breeze, the orange glow of the lamp inside. I couldn't believe it. This was my home. How could someone else be living here?

An overwhelming sadness filled me. I flopped down on the front steps of the building, wrapping my arms around my knees, hugging myself. I didn't belong anywhere anymore. I felt so alone.

The sound of laughter floated out into the quiet of the dark, July night. I looked up. Across the street, the little Jensen twins were getting their bath, squeals of delight coming through their bathroom window. I'd baby-sat them every other Saturday night since they were ten months old.

"Would you remember me now?" I asked into the darkness. I didn't think so. They were too young to remember someone who wasn't around anymore, someone who didn't call across the street to them and wave when they were out playing.

I knew I was feeling sorry for myself, but didn't I have a right? Wasn't I taken away from all my friends? And didn't Joey wreck my room? And didn't he break the lamp Grandma gave me?

I sat on the steps feeling the anger and the hurt and the loneliness, letting it all mix together, filling me up inside. I sat there a long time, not thinking, just feeling, listening to the Jensen kids as their bath finished, and they went to bed. And then I cried very quietly. My anger was gone. I missed Dad. I didn't want him worrying about me. I knew I should call him. I reached into my pocket to see if I had enough change to call. But then he was there.

It was like telepathy or something. Dad's old brown car pulled up to the curb in front of the apartment just like it used to. The car door slammed, and I watched him walk with hunched shoulders around to the steps. When Dad hunches his shoulders with his hands in his pockets and walks with his head bent like that, I know he's not angry. He's just worried and being serious and wanting to talk.

"Thought I'd find you here," he said, and sat down on the steps beside me. He folded his arms across his chest. "Must be eight miles from the house to here. A good hike." He cleared his throat. "I brought you a sandwich. Pam made it. She said you'd be hungry. Here." He took a slightly squashed, foil-wrapped package out of his pocket. "It's a little dented, but I'm sure it's still good."

I don't know why I started to cry again, but I did. Gobs and gobs of tears. Dad put his arms around me and pulled me close to him. And I pressed myself against him as hard as I could. It felt so good being held by him, just like he used to. I clung to him and when I finally stopped crying, I asked, "Why does Joey hate me so much? Why did he do that?"

"Kate, that's difficult to answer. In fact, I don't think I know the answer." He gazed across the street at the apartment house with its screened-in porches. "My guess is that it doesn't have anything to do with who you are as a person, or with who I am for that matter." Dad turned to look at me. "I don't know if you've noticed but Joe's not too thrilled with me either." He smiled but I knew he didn't feel good about it.

"Pam says he never got over his dad dying, and that he's still all tied up inside about it. How or why all that comes out against you I don't know. I guess that's not much of an answer is it?"

"Linda said something like that too, about Joey missing his dad, and not wanting things to change." Dad was rubbing my back and looking at me in that thoughtful, analyzing way of his.

"Maybe that's not too different from you sometimes missing your mother. I know you do. I've wished at times that things could have worked out better, for your sake, and for mine too. But they didn't. Your mother loves you." Dad pulled me closer. "She knows what you need, and hopes you'll get it from me or someone. She just doesn't think she can give you, and do for you, what she thinks a mother should. But remember, she loves you. And maybe when you're older, she'll talk to you about why she left."

I was crying, the tears dropping onto my bare arm. "It hurts, Daddy. It still hurts."

"I know baby, I know." He held me tight, and I could hear him crying along with me. "And I guess Joe hurts inside too."

After a long silence, he sighed and began stroking my hair. "Somehow, Kate, I want us all to be happy. Maybe that's not possible, I don't know, but I'd like us to try."

"I've been trying, Dad. I really have. Today, just hurt. It made me feel like I didn't belong with the rest of you."

A smile broke across Dad's face. "You belong very

much. We need a whirlwind like you to keep us from rusting our bottoms out. Now let's go on home." He stood up. "We have some painting to do in your room, get it all bright and new again. And then we have to start getting the tents and gear ready for our camping trip." He held my hand as we walked to the car.

"You eat the sandwich while I drive. And when we see a store, we'll stop and get a soda." He squeezed my hand and I smiled.

Somehow Dad made me feel better. I feel close to him again. Maybe I'm not losing him. With Pamela in his life, he seems happier. She's someone to him I guess my real mother couldn't be. And maybe together Pamela and Dad can make a go of it. I'm beginning to hope so.

The Crossing

The Oskeet River:

Kate heard Linda scream as she slid in the mud down the bank. Linda had fallen hard, banging her leg against the ground. Hearing her in such agony, all Kate could picture was the broken bone tearing through her skin.

She pushed herself up as fast as she could and crawled to Linda. There was a stick lying in some leaves. Kate wiped it off and put it between Linda's teeth, watching her clamp down, grinding her teeth into the wood. Lying rigid on the flattened life jackets, Linda moaned in agony.

Kate looked quickly at the splint. Surprisingly, it was okay. She was thankful the bones hadn't moved, but the leg was swollen worse than ever. She knelt and loosened the splint slightly to ease the swelling. Her hands trembled as she worked at the straps. The excitement she had felt at getting close to camp was gone. Things were far from better.

The stretcher pole wasn't broken all the way through, but enough to make it useless. If they were lucky, they were only a couple of miles from camp. But to get Linda there, they still had to carry her those two miles.

Linda wasn't moaning as loudly now but she shivered almost continuously in the cold rain that steadily fell.

Where was Joey? Being so caught up in worrying about Linda, Kate had forgotten all about him. She was starting to stand up to look for him, when a noise like a gunshot went off among the trees. She was so jittery, she jumped. Thunder? No, she shut her eyes and took a deep breath. It was Joey.

She saw him. Thirty yards back along the riverbank, his arms stretched above his head, his hands hidden among thick overhanging tree branches. The noise was one of the branches breaking off. Joey was pulling it with all his might, leaning backward.

Seeing Joey struggling with the tree made her feel better. Right away he had known the only way they could fix the stretcher was to make another pole. Kate smiled. Joey wasn't giving up, and neither would she. Another loud crack and he had broken the branch free. She began hurriedly untying the broken pole from the life jackets. Some of the knots were tight from the rain, and she had to use her teeth to pull them apart.

"I think this is strong enough, Kate," Joey said as he came up dragging the tree branch through the wet grass.

"It's perfect." Kate smiled up at him. "And you're great. You knew exactly what to do. You're turning out to be a real backwoodsman. We won't be able to get you to come home with us."

"Yeah, right. Don't think I'll ever want to see trees or rain again in my life."

The worried expression he wore most of the time came back, pushing the grin off his face.

"How's Linda? When I heard her scream, I knew she was hurt bad and that we'd have to get the stretcher fixed fast. That's why I ran off, you know, to find another pole." He hesitated. "I knew you'd take care of her." Kate felt her face redden at the unexpected praise.

"Her leg's badly swollen, Joey. I'm afraid there might be infection. Somehow, we have to get her to a doctor real soon."

"Move over. Let me help you."

Together, they pulled the broken pole free from the stretcher. Then working quickly, they wrapped the vines around the new pole and through the holes in the life jackets, knotting each vine tightly so the pole was fastened securely to the jackets. When they finished, the stretcher looked as strong as ever, which Kate knew didn't mean much considering what had just happened.

After making sure that Linda was lying safely on the life jackets, they lifted the stretcher. Maybe the new pole weighed more, or maybe she was just more tired, but the stretcher felt heavier. Kate made sure she had her footing, and waited a second or two for Joey to get his; then they started.

They had been carrying the stretcher now for so long,

it seemed to Kate like it had joined them permanently to each other. She realized that as bad as Linda's broken leg was, having to carry her on the stretcher was forcing Joey and herself to work together. She thought that if there was any good in all this, it had to be that. But it wouldn't mean anything if they didn't get Linda to a doctor in time.

A half an hour later, as they rounded a bend in the riverbank, Kate saw through the rain what looked to her like the small beach off their campsite. Because it was still a good way off, and the rain was so heavy, she wasn't sure if her eyes were tricking her. Maybe I want to believe it so much I'm seeing things, Kate told herself. She didn't say anything to Joey. There was no good in getting his hopes up and then disappointing him if she was wrong.

But even if it wasn't the beach, Kate knew she needed to start looking for a spot to cross the river. Joey had most likely forgotten that their camp was on the other side, on the point of land just north of where the river branched. She wasn't going to remind him until she had to. He would be scared when he found out, but they didn't have a choice. They had to cross the river, and they had to do it sometime soon. The river was at its shallowest along this stretch.

While they trudged through an open area of high grass, Kate scanned the river for the best spot. No place would be completely safe, but the shallower the better.

With the river rising, there was a real risk of being washed away, swept down into the rapids again. But they had to take the chance if they were going to get Linda to help.

Kate could now see the beach more clearly, and was almost sure it was where they had launched the canoe. But yesterday, it had been quiet and peaceful, with gently sloping sand. Now, the wind and the water were tearing the beach apart. With the river running high, it wouldn't be long before the point of land and their campsite were flooded.

The trees, leaning downriver, thrashed back and forth under the force of the hard-driving wind and rain. The thunder and lightning had passed, but the storm clouds still hung dark and merciless over them.

Searching carefully, Kate saw what she was looking for: a widening of the river, which meant shallower water. She hoped it would be shallow enough to wade across. Farther up, the river was narrower, and the current more powerful and dangerous.

Here, at this widening, the river looked to Kate to be no more than waist deep, not so deep that they couldn't cross. The current would still be strong. But as long as they kept their footing and fought against the pull, they would have a good chance of getting to the far side. They would have to float Linda across on the stretcher, holding it between them, but the buoyancy of the life jackets would help keep her afloat.

When they reached the spot where she intended to cross, Kate stopped and shouted over her shoulder to Joey, explaining what they had to do. He went instantly pale. His hands tightened on the stretcher poles until his knuckles were as white as his face. For a second, Kate thought he would refuse to go. But then, with his lips pressed tightly together, he nodded. He knew they didn't have a choice, not if Linda was going to get help.

"We'll go slowly. The current is pretty fast so lean into it, and keep your feet on the bottom. Slide your feet, like we did yesterday crossing the stream. Okay?"

"Yeah, let's get it over with."

Kate started down the slope and out into the river. They went slowly, the cold, muddy water rising up their bodies the deeper in they went. It didn't take Kate long to see she was wrong about the depth of the river. A third of the way out, it was already at her waist and, what worried her more, at the middle of Joey's chest. If it got much deeper, the current might pull him off his feet. She could kick herself. She was so tired she had forgotten how much shorter Joey was.

"Joey, if we get knocked down, hold onto the stretcher," Kate yelled back to him. She wasn't sure he heard. The noise of the river surging around them was louder than it had been up on the bank.

When Kate looked back a minute later, the water had risen up to Joey's armpits. He was straining to stay on his feet. She knew he couldn't last. They would have to turn back.

"Joey, we better go back! Slowly start—"

"Kate!"

He'd slipped under. She couldn't see him. Kate felt panic racing through her. Where is he? Then, she saw him. He was still holding on to the end of the stretcher, just as she had told him to do.

She didn't have time to yell to him. The force of the river was whipping them around in a fast circle. Knowing she was going to be yanked backward off her feet, Kate squeezed the stretcher poles as tightly as she could. A second later, her legs were swept out from under her.

Kate turned to face the stretcher and Joey, changing her handholds carefully. The current was carrying them along too fast. Her heart was thumping crazily, but there was no time to think about being scared. Things were happening too fast.

"Joey," Kate yelled. "Kick your feet! We'll swim the stretcher across."

Joey started kicking instantly, frantically, causing the stretcher to wobble. Caught off guard, Kate had to kick as hard as she could, matching Joey's kicks until the wobbling stopped and they straightened out. They had to move together, or they would end up on the rocks downriver.

They were moving across. But not fast enough. The

river was narrowing, picking up speed. If they didn't stop the current from sweeping them along, they would end up miles away from camp, if not worse. Kate knew she had to get her footing again on the bottom. Reaching her legs down, she wasn't expecting to touch, but she did. Sand and stones squished under her toes.

"Joey!" she yelled. "See if you can get your feet on the bottom!"

Kate watched Joey paddle down, searching with his feet, holding tightly to the stretcher poles. He found it, then lost it, his legs floating up with the current. He tried again. Kate was sliding her feet sideways along the sand and stones, moving as best she could with the current, not wanting to be pulled off-balance by the rush of water.

"Kate! I have it! I'm touching the bottom!" Joey yelled, sounding amazed with himself.

"Okay. Try to walk to the bank! Dig your toes into the stones!" Kate yelled back.

They leaned forward toward the row of trees that were fifty feet from them. Kate kept her eyes glued to one small pine tree doubled over by the wind and rain, and forced her body through the water.

The stretcher worked against them, the river catching at the life jackets, trying to tear them apart. Glancing at Linda, Kate saw that her face was still clear of the water. That's all that matters, she told herself, that and just getting across the river.

They were making it. The water was now down to her waist, and the small pine tree was still in front of her.

"We're going to make it!" Kate called excitedly to Joey.

He smiled back tired but happy. He opened his mouth to holler something. But that fast, he was gone. His hand slipped from the stretcher pole and the river swallowed him. Just once Kate saw his feet kick to the surface a dozen yards away. That was all.

Kate was frantic. Joey was gone. The stretcher with Linda on it was pulling away from her. She quickly changed her position, grabbing the stretcher in the middle. Then, pulling as hard as she could, she dragged it toward the riverbank. She had to get Linda across before she could look for Joey. She had to get Linda up on the bank. Her head was pounding.

From Kate Evans's Diary:
SATURDAY, JULY 7

This morning, Linda and I packed Dad's old Chevy van, the one he and I always use to go camping. It was early, and Bear was running around the yard, knowing in some strange animal way that he was going out into the woods with us. We had all gotten up at five-thirty to pack and eat and get going. Pamela was inside the house cooking breakfast.

Joey was still avoiding me. He'd been avoiding me ever since the night I arrived back at the house with Dad. He'd come to me then with Pamela and apologized, but he wasn't real. I could see he didn't mean it. He hung his head and had to be shaken by Pamela to say anything. You could see that Pamela was making him apologize, cause he sure didn't act sorry.

And this morning, he was dragging around the front yard. He didn't want to go camping. He made that really clear.

"Hey Joey, come on! Get your sleeping bag and put it in the van! Don't leave it there on the ground," Linda shouted. She was still angry with him for causing trouble. That night had been the first time I'd seen her angry with him. I mean really angry.

"I'll put it in when I want to," he snapped back at her.

I wanted to tell him he was acting like a little kid, but I kept my mouth shut. Me saying anything to him wasn't going to help. That I've learned.

Linda climbed out of the van. Her face was red she was so angry. I'd never seen her so worked up. She walked quickly over to where he was leaning against Pamela's Volvo and grabbed his arm.

"Now, you listen to me, Joey Morgan! You've done enough! You make this trip miserable and I'll never forgive you!"

Joey looked hurt. Linda meant a lot to him and to have her talk to him that way bothered him. He looked at the ground and kicked a piece of gravel across the driveway.

"Bug off! Leave me alone!"

"Come on, Joey! We'll have fun." I opened my mouth and said it before I realized I was talking. I just didn't want any bad feelings between them. And I didn't want to be the cause of it. Again, stupidly I thought I could make things better.

"Yeah sure, it's going to be fun. Only nerds like you want to swat bugs all day, and get chased around by bears."

"There won't be many bugs. And we won't see anything wilder than a raccoon. It'll be perfectly safe. We can swim and fish, and I'll teach you how to canoe."

"Great! I'm going to swim with a bunch of fish and paddle around in a tin can. Lots of fun! And then on top of everything, I get to look at your ugly face."

"Joey! Stop being nasty to Kate! Haven't you been mean enough?"

"But I don't like her!" he shouted at Linda. "I hate her! I don't know how you can be buddy-buddy with her. She's a stupid nerd!" He screwed up his face. "I hate camping! It's going to be boring and stupid!" He kicked the car tire and stomped away.

"Terrific," I said. "I always wanted to be hated."

Linda, her face all flushed, put her hand on my arm.

"Don't let him upset you, Kate! He's just scared."

"Scared?"

"Yes, he's scared to be going camping. He's never done it before. He's never even slept out in the back-yard. And you know how boys are. They have to know it all and be better at it than girls. He doesn't like it that you're able to canoe and swim, things that scare him."

"I guess that means he's going to keep being nasty."

"Most likely." Linda was blinking back tears. "I so much want this camping trip to be happy, if only for Mom and your dad."

As much as we might both want it, somehow I don't think it's going to work out that way.

The Oskeet River:

*H*olding on to the side of the stretcher, Kate dragged Linda out of the water, pulling her up the slope of the bank. She pulled Linda up high enough for her to be safe for a little while. With the river rising fast, Kate knew she couldn't leave her for long. She had to find Joey quickly, if she could find him.

Kate ran along the dirt and stones at the edge of the river, looking for Joey. The rain had slowed, so she could see a lot farther out over the water, but there was no sign of him. With the river flowing high and fast, it could have carried him hundreds of yards in the time she was getting Linda up the bank.

As Kate forced her way through a wet tangle of bushes, impatient that it was slowing her down, she saw him. He lay on his side, his hands latched onto a bush, his body still out in the river, the water tugging at him, waiting to pull him back. Somehow he had made it, but it might not be for long.

Kate ran as fast as she could along the bank. He saw her and tried to pull himself up, but slipped back exhausted. She got to him and grabbed his arm.

"Joey, are you hurt?"

He shook his head. "No," he managed to say.

As he tried to push himself up onto his knees, Kate caught him around the waist and pulled him up the bank. He lay on the ground with his eyes shut, gulping air.

"Are you sure you're okay?" Kate asked anxiously. All he could do was nod.

"You scared me to death. One second you're there, the next second you're whizzing off downriver."

Joey opened his eyes. "Scared me too." He was breathing better. "I was sliding my feet along the bottom." He paused and took a deep breath. "Then suddenly there wasn't a bottom. A big hole. I went down and lost my grip on the stretcher. The next thing I knew I was doing somersaults. I knew I was going to drown if I didn't get my head up somehow. I just held my breath and kicked my feet and beat at the water with my hands. I got to the surface somehow and saw the trees and just kept kicking.

"I thought I wasn't going to make it, thought my lungs were going to burst. I'd risk taking a breath and hold it for as long as I could. And then, when I finally thought I couldn't keep going on, that I was done for, my feet touched the bottom. I dug in with my toes and pushed and pushed against the stones until the water got shallower and easier." He looked at her. "I finally made it."

Kate was so glad to see him that for a long moment

she just looked and looked at him. She saw that his muddy, bedraggled shirt no longer said GET OUT OF MY FACE. Kate felt like she was going to cry. She knelt down and hugged him.

"Come on, let's get Linda back to camp." She was sick of the river. She wanted the three of them to be safe and dry.

When they reached Linda, the river was already up to the stretcher. It was rising faster than Kate had thought. Linda was awake again but weak. Kate knelt beside her and touched her forehead. She felt cool. The rain had broken the fever.

"We're almost there, Linda. We'll get you to a doctor soon." Kate squeezed her hand reassuringly, then looking across the stretcher, said to Joey, "How about we get to camp and a dry towel?"

"Now you're talking!" Joey danced around to his end of the stretcher. "Let's boogie!" They picked up their makeshift stretcher with Linda on it and started off.

They had lost a lot of ground crossing the river. Kate figured they had maybe a mile and a half to hike back. And through the dense thickets along the edge of the water the going was slow. It took them nearly two hours to push through to the beach near their campsite.

Even with the rain pelting down harder now than ever, they were ecstatic. They hurried over the now tiny beach and into the trees. Kate wanted to see her dad badly. She wanted to run as fast as she could to him. But she made herself stay with Joey and Linda and the stretcher that had bound them all together for so long.

The camp was through the trees in a large clearing off a dirt access road. Kate could see the tents. She was so happy she started to cry.

"Dad! Pamela! We're back!" she shouted.

With all the rain, Kate knew they couldn't hear her. She waited until she was fifty feet away then called again.

"Dad! We're here! We need help with Linda!"

No answer. Everything was quiet. Her excitement sank away. Kate began to notice things. The van was gone, and the other canoe. The tents were tied shut. Nothing was out. The camp was deserted. No one was there.

The Oskeet River:

*W*here are they? Where is everyone?" Joey asked, his voice rising in distress.

"I don't know." Kate forced herself not to cry. She couldn't let her dejection overwhelm her.

"Come on, help me open the big tent and get Linda inside out of the rain. Then we can figure out what to do."

They undid the door ties and carried Linda in where it was dry. The tent was her dad's and Pamela's. Their sleeping bags and hiking packs were stacked neatly in a corner. Either they were coming back soon, or they were forced to leave before they had time to get everything. Kate found a couple of towels and dried Linda as well as she could.

"Let's see if we can find some dry clothes and our ponchos."

They went back out into the rain and across the clearing to their own tents. Inside the tent she shared with Linda, Kate saw that her dad or Pamela had packed up her clothes. It took her a few minutes to undo the bags and find what she needed.

By the time she had dried down and changed, she

could hear Joey sloshing across the clearing. She toweled her hair once more, enjoying how really good her sweatshirt and jeans felt against her skin. Just being dry and warm picked up her spirits.

Kate put on her poncho, wrapped up Linda's clothes and a towel in another poncho, and went out. Joey was waiting by the drowned fire pit, his army green poncho covering him like a pup tent. Dangling from his hand was his trumpet.

"What do you have that for?"

"We don't know where our folks are and they don't know where we are. They may be nearby, right? We just don't know. So I got this idea."

He smiled at her and put his trumpet to his lips. A simply awful rendition of reveille burst upon Kate's ears and filled the clearing. Nothing ever sounded so good to her. She ran to him through the puddles and hugged him.

"What a great idea! Maybe they'll hear us!"

"It's worth a shot."

"As long as they don't think it's a rampaging elephant and run the other way," Kate said.

Joey kicked at her, missing by a yard. He was still laughing when she ducked into the tent to help Linda put on dry clothes. Being dry and warmer made everything look more hopeful.

Kate's good feeling ended as soon as she looked at Linda. Her fever was back. Her head and body were burning up. The rain had kept Linda cool. Now that she was dry, the fever was back. She was unconscious again, her lips moving, mumbling something Kate couldn't understand.

Kate changed Linda down to her waist. She didn't want to move her leg so she left the wet shorts on her. Kate doubled over the dry towel she had brought and put it between Linda's back and the wet stretcher.

Kate knew they couldn't stay in camp and wait. For all she knew, the ranger might have forced her dad and Pamela to leave. They might not be back for days, not until after the river dropped. And Linda had to get to a doctor. Kate covered her with her poncho, tucking it gently around her, then went outside.

"Joey," Kate called. "Linda's worse! Her fever's back! We can't wait here. We have to get her to help."

Joey was standing at the entrance to the clearing, on the dirt road. He had been blowing his trumpet every few minutes. He now came hurrying over to the tent.

"It must be miles to the main road. Wouldn't it be better to stay here? Somebody's bound to hear the trumpet and come. And here we can keep her dry."

"Joey, we can't take the chance! They may have gone hours ago. We just don't know." He was worried again, biting a fingernail and looking wishfully toward the road.

"I saw a jug of juice and a cooler with bread and

cheese and fruit. We better eat something quickly, and make some sandwiches to take with us. Come on."

He followed Kate back to the tent where she made some sandwiches and put them in a knapsack. While Joey gobbled down bread and cheese, Kate washed Linda's face with a wet towel, trying to cool her down.

"You're right, Kate. We have to keep going."

"Yeah, I think so. Let's see how far we can get before it gets dark."

Kate stuffed half a sandwich into her mouth and stood up. A sandwich even eaten fast never tasted so good to her. It had been so long since she had eaten, she had forgotten how hungry she was. As she stood at the open tent flap, her legs started shaking, telling her she was also very tired.

With the knapsack on her back, Kate bent down and got into what had become an old, familiar position. Joey put his trumpet on the side of the stretcher and covered it with a corner of Linda's poncho. Then, together, Kate and Joey lifted the stretcher and carried it out of the tent. The rain was falling as hard as ever.

They started up the dirt road that was now mud. Off to Kate's right the beach was gone, completely covered by water. It wouldn't be long now she knew before the river flooded the camp. It was just as well they were leaving.

They didn't know what was ahead; maybe they would find parts of the road washed away. But for now, the road was a lot easier to walk on, even with the mud, than the riverbank had been, and they made better time.

They walked as quickly as they could, stopping every few minutes for Joey to blow his trumpet. By now, Kate didn't have much hope of anyone hearing him, but it was the only thing they could do besides walking down the road.

Kate felt like they had been walking and carrying the stretcher forever. Her arms and shoulders ached. She was starting to drag her feet, she was so tired. The initial excitement of getting to camp was gone. They had miles and miles to go before they would get to the main road.

Kate looked over her shoulder at Joey. She could just see his mouth and nose, the rest of his face was lost in the poncho's hood. Funny, Kate thought, but he doesn't seem like a brat to me anymore.

"Hey, Joey," she called to him. "I must be getting weird. I think I'm getting to like you. I think I'm actually going to miss being with you like this."

His face broke into a smile. "You are getting weird. But you know, I think I'm weirding out too cause I'm getting to like you. Two weirdos liking each other. We've been out here too long." They both started to laugh. It felt good to Kate to be able to laugh.

"If we ever get back home, you know what I'm going to do? I'm going to—" Kate stopped. She heard something through the rain, something very faint. She heard it, then she didn't. She started walking again, straining her ears and staring down the long, shadowy road that stretched ahead of them.

"Do you see something?" Joey shouted.

"I thought I heard something. Most likely the wind. But how about we stop and you blow your trumpet again."

While Joey screeched away on his horn, Kate kept her eyes on the end of the road that she couldn't really see. There was nothing. It's just me dreaming, she told herself. But then, when Joey stopped blowing, she heard it again, faint, but she was sure she heard it. And she did see something, something very tiny far down the road, a speck of something. It was moving, a flickering, dark color moving in and out of the shadows, coming toward them.

"Joey, do you see it?"

"See what?"

"Come on, let's go. There's something way down the road."

Kate felt excited as they hurried to lift the stretcher. Maybe, just maybe, somebody's coming to help us, she thought. But then, as quickly as she had gotten excited, a sick feeling came over her.

What if the weather was driving animals down from the mountains, animals like the timber wolves she had seen during the storm? What if it was one of those wolves? What if a wolf was tracking them? Kate laughed. She was being silly. Timber wolves tracking them? Come on, Kate, she said to herself.

But if it wasn't an animal, what was it? She knew it wasn't her dad's van or a ranger's jeep. Even so far away, she could tell it was too small for that. As it flashed in and out of the shadows, it seemed to Kate to be running. She stopped and looked back at Joey.

"Let's carry Linda off the road a little."

"Why?" he asked puzzled. "Shouldn't we keep going?"

Kate looked down the road again before she answered.

"There's some kind of animal coming this way, and I don't know what it is."

"Maybe it's a skunk or a raccoon."

"No, it's bigger than that and moving fast."

"What could it be?"

"Maybe a wolf."

"A wolf! Are you kidding me?" Kate shook her head. "Well, let's hide or something."

"The woods are too overgrown along here, Joey. We won't be able to get the stretcher through that tangled mess. But we can at least get Linda off the road and into the shadows. If we keep still, maybe whatever it is won't see us." It was a maybe Kate didn't feel too good about.

After a quick, anxious look down the road, they

carried Linda through the puddles and off the road to a small patch of ground with low overhanging branches. The only other thing Kate could think to do was pick up a heavy stick. Joey held his trumpet against his chest, trying to keep it dry.

Through the branches and the shadows, they watched the animal come toward them. It was close enough now that Kate could see the rolling motion of its run. As cold as she felt, her hands started to sweat around the stick. A wolf, she said to herself. It had to be the way it moved.

As it got closer, Kate's heart beat faster. She made sure one more time that Linda was okay behind her, then she kept her eyes locked on the wolf, not thinking, not hearing anything, just waiting.

As terrified as she felt, Kate was awed by the dancer-like beauty of the animal's run along the road. Maybe the wolf was answering Joey's urgent trumpet call, the blasts of strident notes carrying through the rain and forest to its ears, just like in a Tarzan movie. That's a bunch of romantic garbage, Kate told herself. It's looking for food.

Gripping the stick tightly, Kate held it like a baseball bat. As the wolf sped toward them, she watched for its eyes, waiting, looking for a sign that it saw them, ready to club it when it leapt at them. And then they heard it, its unnerving howl. The howl of a timber wolf.

It was running faster now, straight toward them. Kate

knew it saw them. It was no more than a hundred yards away. She was so afraid, she felt dizzy. She knew timber wolves could be dangerous.

Joey whipped his trumpet up to his lips and blasted down the road. When is all this going to end? Kate asked herself. Will we ever be dry and safe again? The high-pitched notes screeched through the forest. The noise was terrible. It had to scare timber wolves, it just had to.

But the dark shadowy shape kept coming. And in the rain that continued to fall, Kate felt sick to her stomach. Joey stood in the middle of the road and blew his trumpet as loud and hard as he could straight at the animal.

And then the howling started again, answering the trumpet, and Kate knew what it was even before she saw it clearly.

"Bear!" she yelled, and ran down the road toward him. She kept yelling as she ran "Bear! Bear!" She could see him now running toward her, his tongue hanging out the side of his mouth.

Just as Kate got to him, he jumped up, knocking her down, his tail wagging like crazy. She hugged him around the neck and cried, listening to his happy whimpering. Joey came running up.

"Jeez, I never thought I'd be so happy to see this old dog. How you doing boy?" He patted Bear tentatively on the head, and Bear licked his hand.

"Looks like he's happy to see you too. Maybe you'll get to be friends. Bear never could stand your trumpet playing. Remember how he always howls when you play? Sounds like a wolf, doesn't he? He has such sensitive ears. Don't you, fella?" Kate scratched him behind his ears. "But I guess if you didn't play so awful, Bear might not have known it was you. The way he's panting, he must have been running for miles. I wonder if he got lost from Dad and your mom in the storm."

Then Kate saw lights, bright yellow lights way down the road, cutting through the rain and the heavy shadows. It was their van. She knew it was. Her dad and Pamela were coming. They were following Bear. And now they were blowing the van's horn. They saw them. Kate jumped up and down, waving her arms. Joey kept blowing his trumpet. Kate ran to him and hugged him and kissed him, and he hugged her. They were going to be okay. They were going to get Linda to a doctor.

As the van came toward them, Kate felt ecstatic. For the first time in a long time, she felt really happy. Maybe everything will work out, she thought. After all, haven't Joey and I together beaten the river? Couldn't we then beat the stupid problems at home? Well, couldn't we?